A GRAVE DISTURBANCE

An utterly gripping cozy crime mystery

D.M. GREENWOOD

Theodora Braithwaite Murder Mysteries Book 8

JOFFE
Ostara
CLASSICS

Revised edition 2023
Joffe Books, London
www.joffebooks.com

First published in Great Britain in 1998

This paperback edition was first published in
Great Britain in 2023

Cover art by Sasha Alsberg

ISBN: 978-1-80405-885-5

For Carol Rookwood

CHAPTER ONE: ENDING

'This is the happiest day of my life,' Lionel Comfet wrote on his desk jotter. Then, because he couldn't think what to say next, he shifted his pen from his left to his right hand. Since he was left-handed this gave him an excuse for slowing down. 'It gives me great pleasure,' he laboured on, 'to know that I shall never have to see any of you again.' He crossed it out. Surely he could do better than that. He summoned his powers of rhetoric and venom.

'It is as great a pleasure to me as it doubtless is to you to know that we shall never have to set eyes on each other again. I can truly say that in a working life of over forty years, in a diversity of institutions, in this country and abroad, I have never passed a more frustrating time than that which I have experienced here in the service of the Church of England.'

He stopped and read it through. That was more like it. He swapped hands and pressed on with settled purpose. 'Complacency I am familiar with, but not the degree of confident ignorance which I have found here. Arrogance I thought I knew, but not the strutting vanity of the bog stupid which passes for management in the Church of England. Laziness I have met, but the supine lethargy, the brute, bone idleness, the ostrich imprudence practised by those at the cutting edge of the Church's policy-making, these I have never encountered. Incompetence in many forms has, from time to time, crossed my path but nowhere the shambolic, feckless muddle in which I have been expected to work in this office.'

He felt much better. He lifted his head and looked around the pleasant sunlit room with its view of the bright brick spire of the Cathedral Church of All Angels at Giltchrist. Its harsh edges had been softened in recent weeks by a fringe of scaffolding. I am soused and pickled in resentment, Lionel told himself. I have much to be grateful for. The October season was mild, his digestion was excellent. It was Friday, and, for once, there were no weekend duties to interfere with his hobby. Most important of all, he was at last within striking distance of his retirement. This was the third draft of his retirement speech. He was celebrating proleptically. He'd got three months before he could tap into what the Church of England laughably thought of as an adequate pension for ten frustrating years' service. The senior clergy, late in the day, were beginning to cast around amongst their acquaintance for a possible successor.

A working life of forty years ought to add up to something, Lionel thought. The autumn season always brought on these same profitless ruminations about endings and beginnings; the end of the seasonal year and yet the beginning of the academic year: the resumption of normal life as Lionel thought of it. He'd been both a soldier and an academic and been a failure at both. I've never really built up to a grand enterprise, concentrated on one single thing and brought it to a successful consummation. There is no metaphor into which I can cast my life's activity. I have climbed no ladders and hit no targets. But then, what image was capacious enough to sum up a life? Lives were too complex, too meandering, too full of culs-de-sac and interesting side roads for any metaphor to be anything but simplistic. And, after all, he'd come through without positive disgrace.

Lionel returned to the matter in hand. That's the way of it, he consoled himself, this task now, the small good to hand, not some large metaphysical pilgrimage. His only other job today, apart from a meeting with his boss, the Archdeacon, Marcus More, was to pick up the cathedral Provost's wife's guest from the station at six o'clock. What was her name? Bartlett? He glanced at his diary. Braithwaite, the Reverend Theodora Braithwaite. That shouldn't detain him long. He looked again at his jotter. Had he, he wondered, been too harsh in his judgement of the senior clergy?

From behind the door which connected his office with that of his superior, the diocesan secretary, who was also Archdeacon of Giltchrist, the Venerable Marcus More, Lionel could hear the familiar voice saying, 'I do not wish to be interrupted when I'm interviewing a candidate, Reggie. My questioning is cumulative. I employ a catena of linked interrogatives designed to elicit the maximum relevant information from candidates.' I close my case, Lionel thought, as he caught the deep, meaningful voice of the senior clergy talking bollocks.

Archdeacon Marcus More was not a classicist but he had been taught by such in his youth and they had impressed him greatly. He ardently wished to be one of them. But being, even by the standards of the minor public school he had attended, untalented, he'd left without acquiring more than a smattering of the learned tongues. When, however, he felt the call to the priesthood, he'd been offered, as it were, a second chance; he'd seen no reason not to reinvent his persona at the same time as taking orders. So, from theological college onwards, he'd pretended. It had not taken much to impose upon his fellow ordinands. In time his pretence had convinced even himself. He had become one of those figures who had so impressed him when he was fourteen. He specialized in small put-downs on etymology; tiny in-jokes about Propertius, a general air of knowingness and condescension. Lionel was amazed at how successful this was amongst the Archdeacon's fellows, clergy and laymen alike. The Archdeacon's a great scholar, they would tell each other.

Lionel's view was that this persona served the Archdeacon in place of the worldly knowledge which would have been relevant to his post but which he feared to acquire. It was an odd choice, Lionel reflected, for a diocesan secretary to have made. Mostly they needed to be surveyors, accountants or lawyers, or preferably all three. Of course, if they were all three or indeed only one of them, competently, they came expensive, while the Archdeacon came at the relatively modest price of a residentiary canon of the cathedral. In exchange for his modest stipend, he offered a modest performance. Only his appearance was impressive. Tall, with a concave figure to match his concave face, he dominated easily. Some were afraid of him. Lionel had watched his technique. He bullied. He made men obey him. Gradually they came to perceive his lack of quality. Then they despised themselves for their obedience. Thus did he destroy them through their own self-contempt.

Lionel glanced over his composition again. Had he perhaps overstated? Not by a syllable, he reckoned.

Through his half-opened window he heard a car door slam and then a familiar drama.

'Hey! Just a moment, please. I think you've taken my space.'

The protester was male, the respondent female.

'Terribly, terribly sorry,' it said. The tone was vibrant, low, dramatic. Then, with winsome self-deprecation, 'I'm sure you'll forgive me. You see, I'm Kate Wale, Canon Wale, and I'm terribly, terribly late for my time with Reggie Tye. Half an hour max.' The voice had faded as it retreated into the distance.

'But,' said the man's voice, 'but . . .' Clearly it had lost.

Lionel tipped his chair sideways and looked out of the window down on to the roof of a red BMW convertible, this year's model. You won't get round that one, he could have told the disgruntled loser. To him that hath shall be given, as Scripture saith. The Provost of Giltchrist Cathedral, Reggie Tye, lived in the Provost's Lodging across the small lawn to the north of the cathedral, and had, therefore, no use for a parking space. Nevertheless, hierarchy decreed that he should have one. Hence he was wont to bestow the largesse of his space on casual clients. Then he forgot he'd done so and they had to battle it out amongst themselves. It added one more piquancy, as far as Lionel was concerned, to the unquiet tenor of the ways of the close of this comparatively modern cathedral. Lionel recognized, peering from the other car, the pale face of the new community relations chaplain, a man required by his duties to spend his time in the committee rooms of the social services departments of three local authorities (the diocese was long and narrow geographically), and whose pallor reflected this.

Lionel leaned further out of the window and called, 'From him that hath not, even that which he hath shall be taken away.'

The pale one looked up.

'I use a bicycle,' Lionel said chattily. 'Have mine, therefore. Third on the left.' He waved towards the marked space beside the north door of the cathedral and withdrew his head. As he did so he could hear Kate Wale's steps as she passed his door en route to his boss. In a moment they would ring for him to join them. He reckoned he'd just got time to get his stuff down to the secretary before anyone else could get in first. This ought to mean that it got typed by Tuesday instead of the usual four-day wait.

The secretary, Mrs Lure, was at her desk in the outer office. It was a large desk. She had laid it out like an ill-governed kingdom. On its furthest reaches, out of arm's play, and acting as a sort of redoubt, an outer defensive works, were piles of unfiled papers. Mrs Lure never seemed, as others might have done, to find these reminders of neglected work oppressive. She did not care for filing and hence did not do any. What she did like was a good catalogue and there were a number of these for the refreshment of her spirit. They lodged within arm's reach, their bright, glossy (though creased) covers promising a different world from that of work: the worlds, for example, of garden furniture, soft-toy making and home improvements. Nearer to hand lay the first aid box, another road to human contact, full of stale aspirin and unstickable plaster, for Mrs Lure was the designated health and safety officer for the office.

Nearer still on the crowded surface were cracked beakers of dead Biros and pointless crayons. Mrs Lure preferred equipment which had been mended, preferably many times, to the new, which she distrusted. Vases that had been riveted quietly leaked their contents amongst her papers. Mugs with handles repaired with seccotine were hazards when she proffered tea. The WP had to be tapped with increasing sharpness on the side of its head, like an idiot boy in a Victorian novel, before it consented to flicker into life. She felt protective towards it. It needed her. And this was a clue to her nature. Veronica Lure was motherly. Cups of tea would appear unasked for at the elbows of surprised colleagues. Tiny pieces of very old cake sat upon paper doilies to tempt those in need of sustenance. Mrs Lure liked gratitude and was prepared to punish people if they did not supply it fast enough or in large enough doses. Lionel was not alone in finding himself thanking her profusely for performing the smallest of her most ordinary duties.

As her desk, so her life, or, anyway, her working life. Lionel sometimes wondered who had first employed Mrs Lure and on what grounds. What possible competence had they detected in her? Her genius was for misdirecting. She brought together in the same room at the same time people who should at all costs have been kept apart. She put into carefully prepared envelopes exactly half the papers intended for them. Mail marked 'Private and Confidential' she opened; more normal envelopes were left honourably untouched. It was impossible to correct or aid Mrs Lure. She had no understanding that there was any way of doing things other than the path she had embarked upon. She would gaze cross-eyed and cross-armed, bemused, at anyone who attempted to redirect her efforts, wait until they had departed and continue on her way unmodified.

The question was sometimes raised amongst her colleagues whether she knew what she was doing. Were her horrendous errors the result of deep malice towards those who paid her or was she, as Lionel himself said, simply dotty? Either way it was often safer to do your own typing and mailing than to allow Mrs Lure to interpose her disastrous self between you and your correspondents. This meant that Mrs Lure had a fair amount of time on her hands. This she deployed in a number of ways not discernibly related to her work. Every now and again she would get up and wander around the building, visiting remote corners as though to reassure them that they were not forgotten. No one was any longer surprised to open a closet door and find Mrs Lure amongst piles of discarded files, carefully ordering the dust-pans in accordance with some deranged scheme of her own.

The other favoured way of spending her generous spare time was in being womanly, warm and maternal. She liked the domestic and insinuated it into even the most austere of her professional contacts. Phone calls were impossibly prolonged, long after any business had been transacted. Surprised lawyers would be asked how the kiddies were; MPs and senior clerics the state of their health or their gardens. Mrs Lure's theory was that everyone had an interest and that it was only courteous to ask them about it. If this slowed up professional communication and occasionally obscured it (one cleric who kept rabbits was regularly confused with one who built model trains), this was all to the good. People, in Mrs Lure's opinion, worked too hard. Part of her job, as she saw it, was to help them let up, take a breather, as she jovially put it.

Why had no one sacked her, Lionel had at first wondered. But that was before he realized that none of the senior clergy were more competent than Mrs Lure. Hence her employers found it hard to nail with certainty any deficiency. The imprecision of their instructions, indeed the opacity even to themselves of their own intentions, ensured that a river of confusion flowed from the clergy to Mrs Lure and fused into an ocean of incompetently performed tasks.

Lionel opened the door of her office and poked his head round. Many felt it was wise to expose only parts of the person to Mrs Lure's strong rays. She was a small woman but looked larger because she had a big head. Her bronzed hair was looped and plaited about her long equine countenance in a system difficult to trace. Suffice to say it involved the use of imitation tortoiseshell combs and, on festal days, small ribbons. She favoured shawls and frocks with much pleating, flouncing and ruching, the product, it was rumoured, of her own tiny hand. Her bosom was ample and loose, just the thing for people to cry on. She liked that. She wanted the younger typists to tell her all about it and a surprising number did.

'Mrs Lure.' Lionel was deferential. 'I wondered if you could possibly . . .'

Mrs Lure put her catalogue, *The British Needlewoman*, to one side with the air of one who makes a willing sacrifice for the convenience of a fellow.

'Mr Comfet,' she said and then, to establish the degree of relationship, 'Lionel,' and fixed him with her cold, smiling gaze, so open, so glazed. 'I'm sure we can work something out for you.'

Lionel restrained himself from saying he didn't want anything worked out. All he wanted was a perfectly ordinary pair of letters typed, addressed and sent, preferably to the persons to whom they were written, in the not too distant future. It wasn't a favour he wanted, just a straightforward everyday clerical task for the efficient discharge of which she was paid rather more than he since she'd been in post seventeen years as against his own ten.

'All I want . . .' He cleared his throat and started again. No point in getting across the old bat. 'Just a couple of short ones. To Andrew Seamley at Gainshurst and Father Angel at Cray Martyr. Andrew's your priest, isn't he?' Lionel despised himself for grovelling.

Mrs Lure hooded her protruding eyes and slowly nodded her large head. 'One or two problems there,' she admitted, her tone at once threatening and forgiving. How did she manage that, Lionel wondered.

'What would those be then?' He cursed himself as soon as he'd uttered the question for being drawn in.

Mrs Lure put her finger to her lips, leaned forward so he could smell her rancid breath and said, 'Strictly *entre nous*, there has been desecration.' She brought out the word as though she might have just learned it.

'Who has desecrated what?' Lionel considered that the only way to cut through the mystification, which Mrs Lure brewed like strong tea, was to make for the rock of truth.

Mrs Lure drew back her chin in resentment at his lack of finesse. 'There has been desecration,' she repeated. 'Mr Seamley says it's the warm weather. They come out in the evenings.'

'Rats, bats, dogs, cockroaches?' Lionel tried facetiousness.

'Instead of staying at home and watching telly,' Mrs Lure finished.

'Human beings?'

'Disturbing the graves.' Mrs Lure nodded.

'Those table tombs in St Andrew's churchyard?'

'Right.'

'The warm weather?'

'Unseasonable. For the time of year. You'll have noticed. They lack a youth club.'

Lionel put it all together. 'The local Gainshurst youth, enticed by the mildness of the weather, have been using the table-top tombs in St Andrew's for illicit purposes. Right, well, thanks very much indeed for all that, Mrs Lure. By Tuesday then?' He tapped the letters.

Mrs Lure hated to be pinned down. 'I'll pull out all the stops,' she conceded as she reached for *The British Needlewoman*.

* * *

In the larger office on the other side of the stairwell, the diocesan secretary Archdeacon Marcus More poured tea for his guests, Provost Reginald Tye and Canon Kate Wale.

'Over my dead body,' the Archdeacon was saying as Lionel entered.

Oh, if only, Lionel thought to himself as he smiled his pleasant smile at them all and said, 'Kate, how nice. Provost, I hope you're well.'

The Provost gritted his teeth and produced the rictus of a brave man in pain. If the Archdeacon was concave the Provost was convex. He was corpulent of face and figure. His sparse white hair was soft and strokable like cotton wool as though part of some medical dressing. It was unparted and streamed down from the centre of his scalp like a cap, to fringe his forehead. His large fleshy nose would have looked well on the stage; his full lips were red and pursed as though perpetually sucking a sweet and seeking to retain its juices. His was the persona of a great man in ruin. Only, Lionel reflected, he'd never been a great man, only ever a ruin.

He was, however, physically a big man, an athlete in his youth. Lionel wondered if big men feel more pain than small ones, there being more to do the feeling. The Provost, he noticed, exuded his usual smell of homely medicines. Eucalyptus, methylated spirit, embrocation, cough linctus, arnica and Vicks wafted from him according to his need or the time of year, as though, like Philoctetes, he concealed some suppurating sore about his person. Whenever Lionel met him he was reminded of a mattress from which the stuffing was emerging and the springs were peeping through. Lionel shook him heartily by the hand to see if he could elicit a wince of pain but the hand was flabby and unresisting. He edged downwind from the Provost and turned his attention back to Canon Wale.

Kate Wale was generally admitted to be a striking woman. Today, as often, she jangled and clanked. Ropes of man-made amber ending in a large ebony crucifix decorated her fine neck. Her handbag was suspended from a long gilt chain. Her earrings of linked crosses swept her cheek. Over her woollen, mustard-coloured dress she wore a blue silk tunic embroidered with an eastern motif of pink flowers. The effect was of a Byzantine empress in dishabille, of regalia worn negligently. She was tall. Her dark hair, parted in the centre, swept her shoulders. Indeed, sweeping was something which Kate did a lot of. Her hands swept back her hair and she herself swept across the room to embrace Lionel who, in ten years of frequenting clerical company, had not yet got used to being embraced by comparative strangers in the cause of Christian brother, sister or, nowadays, personhood. Not that Kate was so much of a stranger. He'd been around long enough to see her accelerate from naught to canonry. In ten years the mysterious ladder of Anglican preferment had brought her from deacon's orders to cathedral stall. He'd heard her asked, not altogether charitably, how she'd come to progress so swiftly and she had replied, 'I pray. It's what I do best.'

What Lionel felt she did best was leading people on to expect worldliness and then nimbly nipping up the moral high ground to leave them wallowing below, sullied by their own lack of finesse. It was a ploy he'd seen repeated many times. Parading one's own religiosity, announcing one's own piety without shame or modesty, was what, in Lionel's view, Kate Wale did best. What she undoubtedly had been and, indeed, undeniably was, was a woman, at a time when it was fashionably important for the Church of England to be seen to be promoting women. Quality, in the sense of adequate education or a developed spiritual maturity, was not a criterion the Church had time to apply. Kate Wale was what was to hand and, therefore, what had to be preferred. However, Lionel liked spectator sports so he turned to her with real pleasure.

'Hope you didn't have too much trouble parking?' he enquired solicitously. 'Bit of a squeeze on Fridays.'

'Tucked myself into Reggie's space, all nice and snug.' Kate glowed at him.

The Archdeacon didn't care for conversations which he hadn't initiated and didn't control. They spelt independence of thought, which he was against.

'Tea,' he said repressively to Lionel and placed a mug in his hand. 'And I think we'd better get down to business. Some of us have work to do.'

Since it was unusual for the Archdeacon to put in any appearance at all in the office on a Friday, Lionel inferred that there was important or, anyway, unavoidable business afoot. What that might be he didn't know for sure but the cast assembled suggested buildings in some form or other. The Archdeacon did not believe in publishing an agenda before a meeting or even revealing it to others in the course of it. Neither did he indicate how long he intended a meeting to last. Lionel sometimes wondered if the neglect of these elementary courtesies was deliberate, to keep control of things, or whether these procedures had just never occurred to him.

'What are we meeting as?' Kate smiled at them all. 'Are we Diocese or are we Cathedral?'

'Diocese,' said the Archdeacon.

'Cathedral,' said the Provost.

'May I clarify?' Lionel asked affably. 'Are you meeting as DCBM or CPT?'

'Oh, I never know about letters. It's so boys' gamesish. What do they mean?' Kate said.

'You have a choice of Diocesan Committee on Building Maintenance or Cathedral Preservation Trust,' Lionel obliged. 'Would you like to decide what needs to be done and where and then I'll assign it afterwards?'

Lionel controlled the minutes so everyone knew that in the end that was a sensible way to proceed.

'You kick off,' said the round Provost Tye to the stringy Archdeacon More.

Since the Archdeacon simply did not attend meetings which he did not chair, the invitation was otiose and a piece, Lionel thought, of clumsy flattery. It always surprised Lionel to observe who was afraid of the Archdeacon and who was not. Lionel, who could after all have been sacked by the Archdeacon, wasn't frightened of him, but the Provost, who could not be, was. It was a species of magic as far as Lionel could see. He watched while the two of them negotiated the rules of engagement.

The question of precedence fascinated Lionel. Who came before whom? Did the Provost of the cathedral rank above the Archdeacon, who was the eyes and ears of the Bishop in the diocese and was also, in this diocese, diocesan secretary, or was it the other way round? In the cathedral the Provost obviously took precedence. Provost and cathedral chapter rule OK. The Bishop himself has to ask leave from the Provost to enter the cathedral even though his throne is there. But outside the cathedral, in the diocese at large where the Provost's writ does not run and the Bishop's does, who then is top dog?

Lionel suspected that here both the Provost and the Archdeacon were torn between two irreconcilable desires: neither wished their personal importance to be diminished, but neither wished to undertake anything which might lead to work. Bit of a poser for them, that one, Lionel thought, as he watched them at play, to see which instinct on this occasion would prevail.

'Well, obviously, it's the cathedral fabric whichever way one looks at it,' the Archdeacon said, shuffling his papers in a decisive sort of way.

Lionel raised his eyes and looked through the window at the subject of their debate. The *Rough Guide to Britain* had described Giltchrist Cathedral as 'possibly the ugliest cathedral in the UK'. It was that 'possibly' which hurt. 'The ugliest' they could have lived with and gloried in since each and every senior cleric lacked an aesthetic sense.

It had been designed by a pupil of Maufe a long way after Guildford. The main architectural feat had been to make brick, purplish and oblong, perform the functions which in England have traditionally been undertaken by stone. Maufe's pupil had never seen Lego but those who came after him had and were reminded of it whenever they looked at his creation. It had its inception at a time of opulence and assurance just before the First World War. It had reached completion in austerity and uncertainty after the Second. Maufe's pupil had begun with the (to his mind) most important feature, the spire, set on its tower 123 feet high. It had been intended as the culmination of what was to be a six-bay nave. As the money ran out, so, decade by decade, a bay had been lopped off the plans until, at the finish, a mere three short bays made up the truncated nave. 'A parable in brick of the decline of Anglicanism,' the succentor was wont to remark as he showed his visitors round.

But, ugly though it was, its bricks unmellowed by time, its proportions at odds with its function, it yet commanded the affection of those who worked in and around it. As a plain daughter in a family of handsome siblings may have her followers, and allowances are made for her, kindnesses offered, so Giltchrist All Angels had its Society of Friends, dedicated to maintaining the fabric, extending the mission and encouraging the dilatory clergy to build up its worship. The Friends worked hard in the face of much clerical resentment. Their chief enemy was the Provost whose distaste for all activity but especially the activity of worship was so pronounced that he was on record as having banned the praying of a second collect at the eight o'clock Eucharist on the grounds that it would lengthen the service.

Lionel gazed at the network of scaffold which was beginning to mount up the tower towards the spire. He was struck by the simplicity of the building methods. Ladders led from one tier to another; a pulley with a bucket on the end took materials up and down, as it must have done when mediaeval cathedrals had been built. The low tech delighted him. It all looked so precarious. Men clambered about aloft, agile and confident, with tools in their belts. One such, whom Lionel recognized, to whom he nodded as he came into the office as one early starter to another, was balancing poles on his shoulder and making his way along the topmost level.

'Money,' said the Archdeacon ominously.

'Vulgar,' pronounced Canon Wale who had plenty of it owing to being married to Leslie Wale of Wale Holdings which had interests in building and land development. 'We must have faith. Prayer will suffice.'

'That's all very well, but I'm not prepared to have the cathedral falling about my ears. Apart from anything else, it's dangerous.' The Provost was peevish.

'Well, where is the money to come from? The Friends . . .' The Archdeacon pronounced the word with distaste.

Lionel reflected on the Friends. Reggie Tye had inherited them from his predecessor, but he had not nursed them. The Provost nagged and blamed but failed to inspire. Lionel, as secretary to the group, had watched relations deteriorate. The Provost didn't seem to realize that the Friends gave their time and money voluntarily, they didn't *have* to support either the Provost's ego or the ugly building. Moreover, Lionel had begun to see that they did not trust the Provost. He wasn't businesslike. He didn't answer letters, he didn't keep accounts, he wouldn't have known a target if it had been presented to him on a plate with a garnish. Many of the Friends knew about these sorts of things. They had been successful in their various spheres. They had begun to recognize that the Provost wasn't.

'Actually,' said the Provost and then stopped. A look of cunning changed his features from their normal flabby lethargy, to give his expression an air almost of intelligence.

'What is it, Reggie?' said Kate. 'Do tell.'

'English Heritage. Sir Derek has been in touch. Provided we can match them pound for pound.' He liked the phrase and so repeated it. 'Pound for pound, they'll give us the first quarter-million.'

'Two hundred and fifty K.' Kate also had the modern parlance.

'How much do we need in total?' Lionel knew the answer to his own question but wanted to inject realism. They'd no more manage to raise such an amount amongst themselves than pigs might fly. He hated the sort of large talk which small men indulged in to keep themselves in countenance.

The Provost glanced at him with real hatred and eased his pain-racked body upright in the Archdeacon's canvas and steel diocesan issue chair. 'Two and a quarter million,' he admitted.

'Lot of money,' Lionel said judiciously as though this might not have occurred to them. 'Where's it to come from?'

'Anonymous donor,' muttered the Provost, without conviction.

'And do you actually have one?' the Archdeacon enquired.

Just for a moment Lionel was struck by the Archdeacon's tone. It sounded as though he was seeking a confirmation, colluding almost in something they both knew and he and, presumably, Kate did not.

'How exciting,' exclaimed Kate. Lionel was reminded of Violet Elizabeth Bott.

The Archdeacon shuffled his papers. 'The last set of accounts from the Friends . . .' he began.

'I always think it's such a one-sided friendship,' Kate said brightly. 'They give and give to the cathedral, time, money, talents, but what does the cathedral give them in return?'

They all thought about this. Then the Provost said, 'A centre of, er, liturgical excellence. A beacon of light.'

The Archdeacon looked cynical. The cathedral wasn't, in the end, the responsibility of the diocese.

'A calm refuge from the hubbub of the materialistic world,' the Provost went on.

Lionel recognized a bit of a sermon he'd heard the Provost preach.

'We haven't got the money to prime the Heritage pump,' the Archdeacon said.

'We've got to get it. We'll never get another offer like this. If we turn it down, if we can't raise the ready, Sir Derek told me quite categorically . . .'

The Provost's mental anguish exceeded, Lionel thought, his physical. Did he really care about that monstrously ugly building? Or was it simply that he couldn't bear to be connected with failure? Was this the Provost's justification for his life? The Provost, who had few talents, who did nothing very well, had invested his emotional capital in a building.

Lionel turned his gaze to the window, towards the high red tower and its scaffold. He'd watched it grow and wondered where the money came from to get even this far. He marvelled again at the courage of those who mounted the bending ladders to reach the highest platform. He watched as the tiny figure of the man with the poles on his shoulder approached the end of the platform, turned to descend the next ladder and pitched forward, his arms waving into nothingness and the poles hurtling towards the ground.

'Oh, God,' he said as he started from his chair, 'oh, God.'

CHAPTER TWO: MEETING

'This is green belt country,' Lionel said, waving his hand through the car window at the litter-strewn hedgerow. An iron bedstead peered from the ditch, its mattress sprouting striped fungus.

'Have you noticed,' he pressed on, making conversation for this difficult woman, 'how fungus accommodates itself to its surroundings? If you've got a wood full of empty Coke tins, you get fungi in the shape and with the patina of Coke tins. If you've got rusting iron kettles . . .'

'Yes,' said Theodora. 'Yes, I had noticed it.'

They sped through a countryside which looked like a painting that had been tampered with, as though a TV set had been painted into the *Mona Lisa* or *Déjeuner sur l'herbe* had a tower block or two added to it. Two, at least, civilizations, rural and industrial, contended. Thin ponies grazed in fields which were truncated by car breakers' yards; small plantations of cabbages and pick-yourself beans stretched as far as the local authority environmental recycling plant. This was green field factory site land; the dream, the ideal only of purblind developers who themselves lived elsewhere. Surreal, at moments, in its unexplained monuments, it startled the traveller into unexpected connections. A pillbox of indestructible concrete opened its wide, blank eye upon an enclosure stacked with upturned cast-iron bathtubs through which hardy clumps of ragwort and willow-herb, bramble and golden rod confidently grew, knowing this to be their very own terrain. Trees were stunted, the grey grass was frayed. Ownership had long since seeped away into the polluted ditches. Notices proclaiming 'Shooting in progress' or 'No dumping' referred to no reality. If there were dangers they were of a more modern kind. The land had been mined for cement's constituents and what had been taken from it had not been put back. Every now and then, the earth grumbled and fell in on itself. Fissures appeared overnight and after heavy rain, creating apertures, entrances to the underworld, as it might be, into which the living might disappear but from which, too, dead horror might reissue.

Suspended between a motorway and a bypass the country harboured little wildlife. The deafened hedge birds had left long ago. The odd fox, more urban than rural, a dustbin scavenger in the adjacent villages of Gainshurst and Cray Martyr, crows whose ancestors had known the fields when they were farms and a persistent, nervy rabbit were all that remained.

As the land so the people. It was not a place where human beings flourished; they did well to survive, in shacks and caravans, in abandoned railway carriages and demountables, in ill-built and subsiding terraces. All the dwellings looked temporary but the temporary in this land lasted, as though the human spirit clung on but felt it was not worthwhile to construct anything enduring.

Theodora Braithwaite, a woman in her thirties in deacon's orders in the Church of England, surveyed the landscape through the smeary windows of Lionel Comfet's car. It was a Morris Minor, thirty-five years old. It had real red leather upholstery and moved like a tiny tank down the middle lane of the motorway while more modern vehicles careered past on either side. It looked small from the outside but Theodora, who was six foot one, did not find herself cramped for legroom. Everything in it worked but effortfully, as an old person might move. The windscreen wipers ranged stiffly in soldierly fashion back and forth across the darkening sky to cope with the sudden shower of warm autumnal rain. Lionel drove very correctly, as though he'd just passed his test. Every now and then he had to signal. Before he did this he looked in his huge rear mirror, wound down the window with a physical effort which could have opened a lock gate, moved a large switch on the hub of the steering wheel, and stuck his arm out of the window. When he'd completed the turn, he did all the actions again in reverse order. Theodora was fascinated. Here was real driving, nothing slovenly or neglectful.

After completing one such sequence, which took them off the motorway and onto a slip road of potholes, lightly joined together by disintegrating tarmac, Lionel took up the conversation once more. What on earth had induced her to venture to this unalluring part of south-east England, Theodora wondered.

'Have you known Susan Tye long?' Lionel felt he was a host as much as a driver.

'We were at Cheltenham and then Oxford together. After that we rather lost touch.'

Lionel was happy. He'd got the information he wanted painlessly.

'So Susan married into the Church but you serve it professionally.'

'I suppose that's true. But I don't think of the Church as a profession somehow, I mean like the law or the services.'

Lionel nodded his head rapidly up and down. 'It's not something one does in addition to anything else and for the money. It's the whole of one.'

Theodora detected a sympathetic intelligence. Many with whom she worked would not have taken her point. She glanced at the small figure beside her. He was dressed like an old-fashioned prep-school master in a pepper and salt tweed jacket with leather at the cuffs and elbows and faded fawn cords. His long, rather lugubrious face reminded her of

Labradors she had known. His hair, which was plentiful and neatly cut in a military shape, looked as though it had been fair but was now grey. She noticed a tic in his left cheek, not pronounced but suggesting a nervousness at odds with his ordinary appearance. There was, she detected, some strain, some reticence. He imitated normality with deliberation, as a drunk might act sobriety, over-conscientiously. What was he concealing or suffering? How old would he be?

'I'm just about to retire,' Lionel said with pride. 'I've made it.'

'Did you doubt that you would?'

'Now and again.'

'What do you do in the diocese?'

'I chauffeur the Provost's wife's guests about.'

'And?'

'My title is Assistant brackets Lay brackets Diocesan Secretary.'

'Why the "lay"?'

'The diocesan secretary is also an archdeacon.'

'It never works.'

Lionel was aware of a kindred spirit. 'How very true. You obviously know about dioceses.'

'I've worked in a couple.'

'And you're in orders?'

'Deacon's, yes.' Theodora thought, the next thing he'll ask me is if I'm going to be priested.

Lionel had to work with all sorts. He wasn't going to set up any antagonisms which he didn't have to, but he needed to know all the same. 'Will you be priested?'

'No,' Theodora said, interested to see how far he'd push.

'Because?'

It was too complicated, too intuitive indeed, for Theodora to go into details. She considered which strands of the argument would be most intelligible to her companion. 'It's the universal catholic thing. It cuts us off from other bits. We all ought to go together or not at all. We can't just make it up as we go along. Tradition and order.'

'Right.' Lionel's tone didn't signify that he agreed, just understood and perhaps respected. 'And are you in work?'

'I'm curate at St Sylvester's in Betterhouse, south London. On the river.'

'Ah, Geoffrey Brighouse and Gilbert Racy. A most interesting set-up.'

'You know it?'

'Well, it's not in our diocese, of course. But Racy has a national reputation.'

Theodora considered the tic in Lionel's cheek. The Reverend Dr Gilbert Racy ran the St Sylvester Foundation in a Victorian villa next door to her parish church. It catered for people seeking healing for mental illness within a Christian ethos. Had Lionel been a patient?

'So ambition, success, isn't your thing?' Lionel ventured into the personal.

Theodora considered. It wasn't a question she was often asked. Those who knew her well took it for granted that she wasn't. Those who did not know her well, but were of her age, assumed that the Church had a career structure like any other profession and that she would want scope for her talents and would therefore expect to go on and up. Those, on the other hand, who knew the Church and knew there were no systems in it for any such thing to happen, assumed she would not. 'I suppose I'm less a ladder person than a task one. I like to perfectly accomplish the small tasks to hand rather than be successful in a great enterprise, a top of the ladder person.'

'"Who sweeps a room as for thy sake",' Lionel quoted.

'Exactly so. And Herbert had to wrestle with ambition. All those courtiers sniggering when he changed his clothes and left court. It makes him much more human and his spiritual gains the greater and more convincing. How about you?'

Lionel grinned. 'I think it's true to say I've failed at everything I put my hand to. I've missed targets and failed to scale ladders.'

'You don't sound too depressed,' Theodora said.

'I've acquired one or two skills on the way which give me pleasure. And it's when I look at the successful that I thank heaven.'

'It's diocesan office life that has soured you,' Theodora said with sympathy. 'No greater set of rogues and layabouts.'

'They do so want things on the cheap without acquiring the skills which would give them the right to be taken seriously. They want to tell governments how to govern and administrations how to behave but have so many beams in their own eyes they can't begin.' He paused, considered that the conversation had got too serious and started again. 'Do you know Giltchrist?' he asked in his pleasant way, trying, as he felt was his duty, to distract his guest from the dreariness of lines of council houses through which the secondary road was leading them.

'No, that's more or less why I accepted Susan's invitation.' Though why, she thought, I should want to leave a flat with a view of the Thames and pastoral work in a parish which fully absorbs me for this desolation, heaven knows. But she did know. In her heart she'd sensed something behind Susan Tye's voice on the other end of the phone, some urgency, some desperation even, to which she had instinctively responded. 'It's a pupil of Maufe's, isn't it?' she asked. 'The cathedral?'

'Pig ugly,' Lionel admitted. 'But it fits its country.' He waved at the houses. 'And it's falling down.' He stopped suddenly, appalled at his words.

Theodora switched effortlessly from social to pastoral mode. Here was someone suffering. Whatever help she could offer, he should have. It was the slightest turn of the head, no more than a concentration of the sympathies, but it gave Lionel courage to go on. He'd resolved he would not mention what was uppermost in his mind to Susan Tye's guest, but in the face of sympathy he sought to heal himself of the horror.

'We had an accident at the cathedral. Chap fell off the scaffold at the top of the tower.'

'When?'

'This afternoon. Three thirty.'

'I'm so sorry.'

'Yes. It was . . .'

Theodora noticed the tic appear in his cheek. Lionel rubbed a hand over it as though it were a physical affliction.

'I felt I knew him. I've watched him climb that scaffold several times every day since they put it up a month ago. I've accompanied him in imagination many a time. Watching him, so sure-footed, so self-possessed, was a sort of therapy for me. I felt if I went up with him in imagination I might overcome what I fear.'

Theodora knew exactly what he meant. 'I used to do that when I was learning to ride, or rather learning to jump, as a girl. To rehearse bravery, to iterate the actions of bravery in the imagination might — indeed does, in my experience — help you to face the real thing.'

'Right,' said Lionel. 'Though I don't think it's courage in general I lack. I had fourteen years in the infantry. I wasn't more frightened there than the next man. And I ride point to point.'

'Not for ninnies,' Theodora agreed.

'But heights get to me.'

The council houses had thinned out and Lionel did some double-declutching to take them down a lane of artisans' cottages. The road led him away from what couldn't be helped. Theodora considered this ordinary man with an outdated career and useless sensitivities and knew he needed to keep talking. He hadn't come to terms with his horror.

'Was he a family man?' she enquired.

Lionel waved his hand at the terrace. 'I only learned who he was after he was dead. The site manager knew all about him. But I realized when he told me I do know the family in a sort of way.'

Now that he'd started talking, Theodora saw what a relief it was for him.

'His name was Lee. Mick Lee. He lived quite near here in Cray Martyr. There are a lot of Lees in Cray. He was married with a son. He has a brother too.' Lionel stopped but then resumed. 'I probably ought to go and see them in due course. On behalf of the diocese,' he ended lamely as though this might be an extraordinary thing to do.

'Yes, of course. Though I suppose the parish priest or the Archdeacon . . . ?'

'Not a chance with the Archdeacon. The parish priest might. Tobias Angel. Well-known eccentric.'

'How does it take him?'

'Keeps odd hours. Late nights, early mornings. Drives out in pony and trap. Smart pony. Sings in public. Quotes poetry, Jacobean mostly. Usual sort of thing.' Lionel was dismissive. Every diocese has one, after all.

Theodora thought that all sounded attractive.

'Was Mick Lee a churchman?'

'Shouldn't think so. Few of his sort are. The family are travellers. But you can never tell. Some boyhood contact, perhaps. Boys' Brigade, choir. The most unlikely do. And travellers like to be buried in holy ground, I've noticed. There are three or four churchyards in different parts of the diocese with travellers' graves going back to the mid-eighteenth century.'

'Travellers don't usually work on building sites.'

'I suppose the modern world has left them without a sphere.' Lionel gestured to the scarred landscape.

'Like many of us,' Theodora agreed.

'What the Lees really know about is horses, or anyway ponies. But you can't make a living swapping ponies in this day and age. Not outside Ireland, anyway. Look.'

They turned a corner and slowed. Lionel dabbed at the windscreen with a hand covered in khaki mittens. 'There's Giltchrist.'

They were on a slight rise on the edge of the village of Cray Martyr. Between them and Giltchrist proper for about three miles the ground dipped and the suburbs became tidier and richer.

Lionel filled his guest in. 'That's Gainshurst in the dip between Cray and Giltchrist.'

About five miles off, the cathedral rose on its mound, artificially enhanced but still justified by geology. Its spire pointed towards the heavens in dark silhouette. The fading light of the October evening, colouring the sky with gold and grey slashes after the rain showers, dramatized an already dramatic building.

'It has presence,' Theodora admitted, 'if not beauty.'

'It fits Ruskin's recipe that good religious buildings can only be built by men of faith. The architect was a fervent Anglo-Catholic. But then he spoilt it rather by committing suicide.'

'An equivocal beginning.'

'And so it goes on.'

Theodora wondered whether he was referring to Lee's death or some more continuous moral atmosphere pervading the place. She'd worked in cathedrals. In her experience they were not mirrors of heavenly harmony.

'Hold on to your hat for cultural contrast,' said Lionel as he let in the clutch and they left Cray Martyr and rolled down the shallow hill towards Gainshurst.

* * *

Kate Wale swung her BMW round the last corner on the road which led from Cray Martyr to Gainshurst. Any minute now she would be sweeping into her drive in Church Crescent in the best part of Gainshurst. She loved making the turn, the controlled abandon, the power, the fluency of the wheel, hearing the gravel crunch under the tyres. It gave her a physical feeling of well-being, of security. Her youth had been a matter of latch keys into a series of terraces in Cray Martyr, big ones when Dad was in work and sobriety, meaner ones when he wasn't. Her schooling had been much the same. She'd started in private schools with eye-catching uniforms in purple and grey when they were in funds, and switched to the local comp, which was uniformless, when they weren't. Kate wasn't sure whether her own attitude to dress, indeed to life, had been formed as a reaction to the fluctuation in family fortunes. What she'd looked for, quite consciously, echoing her frail mother's own dearest wish, was social safety.

Now she was secure. Leslie Wale had done well. Wale Holdings had respectable offices in Docklands and Leslie talked, from time to time, about 'going public' and 'floating'. They'd made the house a statement of their success. He was as proud of her as she was of him. She'd made it; he'd made it. They'd both reinvented themselves. They'd done it together. Why, she wondered. Why had they needed to change? Was it that there was no real place for them to be in the spheres they had started from? They were both, she sometimes thought as she sped past the decayed prefabs of Cray Martyr, and the shiny offensive vans in the lay-bys, they were both, she and Leslie, travellers in their way, just like the Lees.

Kate knew about the Lees. When they had run out of the diocesan office and she had heard from the site foreman the name of the victim, she'd had a vision of Mick Lee as he had been ten years ago when she and Leslie had both been young and they'd been going out together. She remembered how Mick had looked then, like something out of a nineteenth-century portrait of the grandeur of the simple life.

The family had lodged, some in vans, some in council houses, which they adapted to their own lives, on the borders of Cray Martyr and Gainshurst. Alsatians on long clothes lines or heavy clanking chains, their fur rougher than most domesticated beasts', roamed and barked round the untended front gardens. Hens occupied the spare bedrooms. Large ferocious women shouted at unresponsive children. Washing was draped on the hedges and insecure fences, despising the council issue clothes lines. Mick Lee had lived in a van abutting on one of these houses on the edge of Cray Martyr. And now he was dead. She felt a tightening of her stomach as though his death presaged her — their, Leslie's and her — ruin, which was silly.

Kate turned her thoughts away from what she could not cope with. She accelerated round the final bend towards her own strength and refuge. Between the trees of the crescent she could glimpse the high hedges of her house.

When Leslie made his first million, they'd chosen Gainshurst together. It was handy for her for the cathedral and the golf course for Leslie. Everything inside and outside the house they'd chosen together. It embodied the aspiration of both their families. Leslie's mother, in a semi in Cray Martyr off the bypass with a view of the cabbage fields, had held Gainshurst, across the railway tracks, as a constant focus for the elevation of her sons, as ardently as any believer setting their hearts on paradise. Leslie's dad hadn't made it in any of the many tasks he'd tried his hand at and in the end he'd gone to Birmingham, never to be seen again, when Leslie was twelve and his brother was ten. Best thing he could have done, his wife had said. She was competent, started a hairdressing salon on the borders of Cray Martyr and Gainshurst. She changed her accent according to the status of her customers, who came from both communities.

What sorts of values had Leslie inherited? What were the fears and tensions which had been passed on, Kate sometimes wondered as she looked at his pale face on the pillow beside her. He felt as fixed and focused in sleep as he was in life, as though he was thoroughly investigating in his dreams those same financial realities which held him when waking.

Mrs Wale had kept the boys doing their homework by sheer willpower, laid it out for Leslie he'd go into business; got him his first job in the City via the husband of a client. He'd taken it from there and he'd done her credit.

Kate was glad he'd made it. She was glad she'd made it. Making it meant comfort, security, stability. She saw no contradiction between her status as a priest and cathedral canon and her comfortable richness. She wasn't greedy; she took her stipend but never claimed expenses for anything and subsidized the cathedral and its work in dozens of small ways. She thanked God for Leslie's prosperity. It meant elbow room for shopping, but also scope for charity. Indeed she felt that not having to count the change every time was in itself a sort of generosity.

She swung the car through its last turn into Church Crescent. The house was called Tudor Cottage but it was neither a cottage nor Tudor. It had five bedrooms and, by the time Leslie had finished with it, five bathrooms. Three acres of recently landscaped garden surrounded it. It stood in a row of similar houses, all with high hedges on every side, in a road which terminated with the church of St Andrew's Gainshurst.

The house had dark stained wooden beams which had no structural purpose. Inside, the same dark beams ran through the rooms though here they were made of fibreglass. The Jewish widow they'd bought it from had let it go. They'd gutted it and now it looked like 1930s Tudor inside, only new. From her bedroom window Kate could glimpse a small brilliant blue pool concealed behind a trellis of leylandii.

Today as she drove the BMW into the triple garage and let herself in, she felt safe; she was certain of herself. She'd made it. The gates to the drive were on a beam and she flashed her coded ray to close them behind her. The need for security was the only flaw. Times had changed. You couldn't trust people the way you once could. They'd had to put in an alarm after they were done over almost before they'd settled in. The drawback to Gainshurst was Cray Martyr. Sometimes in troubled sleep Kate saw the Martyr hordes slipping like marauding Celts to prey upon the fatness of their Roman Gainshurst plenty. The gardeners, cooks and cleaners who supported the domestic life of Gainshurst lived over the railway tracks and came in of a morning, a recognizable army in Cortinas and battered Sierras, dropped off at nine and picked up in the evening by men with little hair and many tattoos in odd places of their anatomy which gave Kate a frisson in the pit of her stomach. Was it empathy or fear?

Anyway, Gainshurst's employers did their best by word of mouth, by recommendation and assiduous checking of references, to see that their employees were dependable. It was never their maids or gardeners who passed the word round the pubs of Cray Martyr about who was worth what. The trouble Andrew Seamley was having with his churchyard vandals, Kate reflected, stemmed entirely from the youth of Cray Martyr. She recalled the grim mess of broken stone from the desecrated graves littering the churchyard. You couldn't co-exist with Cray men. Basically they were violent. They shouted at each other. They settled their disputes by fighting. The very air of the place smelt sharper and more dangerous than that of Gainshurst.

Sometimes Kate could not help but see the Church as a bulwark against the barbarism of Cray Martyr. It comforted her to look up the crescent and see St Andrew's at the end. The church was fourteenth-century. When it had been built it had been surrounded by sheep. Now it rose from a sea of four-wheel drives. It was convenient for the shops and what the locals called with nostalgia 'the village'. It had prospered with its parishioners. It was a most desirable suburban living. The Reverend Andrew Seamley met its needs admirably. He looked and behaved like Gainshurst's idea of a gentleman. His suits were made by a tailor. His sermons did not disturb the conscience of even the most reprobate. He took an excellent marriage and a serviceable funeral. He never made difficulties about whom he baptized. He was a member of the Rotary Club and the golf club. He had a well-organized team of (mostly women) lay helpers who came in, as he put it to his wife, to do the heavy, which left him free to perform the ceremonial duties.

But as Kate locked the garage even her solid house and her position in a solid institution could not banish the thought of Mick Lee. The death of the scaffolder had shaken Kate. His fall, his ruin, seemed to presage more than just a workplace accident. It was Kate who had used her mobile to summon an ambulance, though it was left to Lionel Comfet, she noticed, to do the rest. The foreman had been white and incoherent. Lionel had got the site manager's number and then the next of kin. The site manager knew enough to get the police. There'd be an inquest. It struck Kate he'd had accidents to deal with before. He wore a suit with a pen in the top pocket as though he wasn't used to one but had to put it on when he reached his elevated position. As though it were a disguise.

Kate knew about clothes, clothes as uniform, as camouflage, as statement, as dominance. Somehow the Church seemed to emphasize clothes and made a point of what it wore. When she'd left school she'd been drawn into the Church almost by chance, though of course nowadays she renamed 'chance' 'Providence'. She'd started with lunchtime services in the City to get a bit of a change from the office. They made a fuss of her. She was young, not obviously neurotic, had useful skills, so they made her secretary of the Lunch Club. She found, after a while, that it filled a number of needs which she would not then have dreamed of calling spiritual or religious. She was curious about people and always eager to help others, with genuine sympathy for those less well endowed than herself. In time it became meat and drink to her. She began to attend confirmation classes. Later she trained to be a pastoral assistant; finally, the Reverend Joe Pulley had suggested she might test a vocation. She'd done one of the 'part-time stay in work and go on retreat' courses where you didn't learn to read the gospels in Greek but did learn a lot about counselling. She was bright, orderly, outwardly confident. Socially, Christianity and the Church of England had enough still to give her a place. Personally, she had no doubt but that God spoke to her man to woman, had a care for her, had a plan for her. As a father might have done if he'd been any good. Her relation to the faith was social and emotional. The untesting requirements of the ordination examination had presented no obstacle. She had been deaconed, worked in her City church as NSM curate and then met Leslie.

He'd appeared one lunchtime. He'd been propped on a tomb in the tiny graveyard attached to Kate's church. He'd said he needed somewhere quiet to eat his sarnies. If he went to the pub he'd spend more than he could afford. He wasn't mean, but he was prudent. He knew about balance sheets; might qualify as an accountant. They'd gone about a bit.

She'd been drawn to his intense, focused ambition; all that energy put into work. He didn't sleep much. But he wasn't dull. It seemed right to marry.

And the lovely consummation had been this wonderful place to live in. Kate mounted to her bedroom. It was her idea of heaven; pink and white everywhere. Thick white carpets covered the floor, white and gilt-painted furniture stood round the walls. White satin was spread over the bed. A vase of late white roses stood on the dressing table. Beside her side of the bed was a white ivory and silver Alternative Service Book given her on her confirmation by the Lunch Club. One of the roses had dropped out of the glass and lay stranded and gasping on the white-painted wood. She thought of the dead man, Mick Lee. Suddenly she wanted Leslie. She wanted him to comfort her about Lee.

She went downstairs to her workroom with its letters and noticeboard; her 'glorious clutter' as she called it with pride. There were notices on her board about the Women's World Day of Prayer and Female Spirituality Circle. Kate looked at the latter with pride. She'd been led to form it. It did so much good, her little group. How much women need to be helped to affirm their identity, to question the male-dominated world, to find comfort in each other, in the Spirit. She picked up the white telephone and dialled Leslie's office.

'Oh, Canon Wale,' said his correct secretary, 'I'm so sorry, Mr Wale's not here. He left an hour ago. There's been an accident apparently at one of our sites and he's had to go and sort it out.'

CHAPTER THREE: ARRIVING

'Only a genius could spend a morning urging grown men in confinement to be trees, mountains, cats and reptiles and not be lynched,' Lionel read. The address at the top of the paper was HM Prison Fordingham. His brother wrote a good letter, he thought. Vincent's description of a recently instituted yoga class and meditation group read well.

> *You'll be interested to know the regular C of E chaplain started off by opposing Miss McGregor's efforts (arguments along the lines of 'nasty foreign stuff'), then he found the movement had been started by an RC nun and the RC hierarchy approve it (more or less). So he started to trot along, laying aside the lace cotta for a snazzy pair of light, oh, so light, grey cords. He doesn't join in (yet) but stands around encouraging. It gives tone, I think he thinks. It must, actually, be quite a difficult chaplaincy for someone like him, colonial, is he, or Irish? Anyway not quite out of the top drawer, as mother would have said, when most of us villains come from the best schools, universities and regiments. Once you've got over the embarrassment, it's really no worse than basic training. So you mustn't, dear brother, brood about me, as I think you are wont to do. 'Sweat it out' was ever your*

motto, wasn't it? Anyway, Father Tobias Angel has a lot of pretending to do on the days he's in. However, he's not all pseud; even if he thinks a bit too much about his public presentation of self, I get the feeling too he's genuinely on the side of us underdogs. There's a great crook here called Elvestone, in for some errors in totting up figures. He knows my old buddy Wale who, he tells me, is married to one of your clergy. Can this be right? I never knew Wale was married, let alone to a rising star. What an odd couple they must be. Or are my stereotypes of women clergy out of date, dear brother? He also reckons he (Wale) is a rather bigger villain than he (Elvestone) himself. Since Wale was a client of mine, I'm not too sure what I feel about this. Wale always seemed to me to be too naive to be a crook, though undoubtedly eager for the profits. However, architects who are gentlemen (yes?) have to mix with builders and developers who are not. He (Elvestone) speaks of her (Wale's wife) with admiration. Do you know her? Thanks, by the way, for The Field, which cheers up more than just me. I mention it to no one but your brotherly self but being confined in glorious autumn weather is actually hell.

Regards, V.

* * *

Lionel folded the letter and put it in his wallet. It took him hours to work up the nerve to read his brother's letters. He felt the same sort of hopeless frustration when he contemplated his brother's fate as when he reviewed the performance of the C of E senior clergy. It was all so damned unfair. The law was supposed to protect the innocent not incarcerate them. In the circumstances, anyway as Vincent had described them, there had been no other possible course of action. No one who knew Vincent could possibly suppose that he would intend the death of another human being.

Lionel listened to the cathedral clock half a mile down the road, striking seven. The wind was in the direction of his lodgings. He looked down the street to where the banner stirred in the breeze. 'Giltchrist Amateurs present *The Mikado* at the Royal 1–5 Oct.' The street had come down in the world and this suited Lionel who felt himself similarly déclassé. It had once been a dignified terrace for upper artisans and said, on its terracotta nameplates high up on the side of the first house and therefore out of vandals' way, 'Honeysuckle Terrace'. Lionel had one big and one little room on the first floor and shared shower and kitchen. He relished, therefore, the revolution in modern living which brought a variety of ethnic dishes to his door several nights a week, delivered by a variety of ethnic cooks. On Monday a deft Pakistani brought tandoori; pizza came to him via an extravert Afro-Caribbean in a red van on Wednesday; a demure pair of Chinese girls cycled round on a tandem bearing a serviceable duck and mixed veg on Friday. The other nights he either went to the pub or patronized the Turks round the corner.

Tonight, however, he was bidden to the Provost's. The invitation was unexpected. At first, when it had been uttered, Lionel had supposed it was the result of the momentary bonding which had occurred in the aftermath of the accident. The Provost had been as shaken as Kate Wale. He had stood about, his large theatrical presence proclaiming his lack of role, while Lionel dealt with the site manager and the ambulance people. Then, just as Lionel prepared to leave the scene, he'd said, 'Miss Braithwaite . . .'

'Yes,' Lionel had said curtly. 'I hadn't forgotten. I'm just on my way to pick her up now.'

'I wondered, I mean, Susan asked me to ask if you'd care to have supper with us tonight. She's having one or two people in to meet Theodora and wondered if . . .' He lacked strength, apparently, to finish.

'Yes,' Lionel had answered. 'How very kind. I'll go anywhere for a free meal.' It was remarks like that, springing from an ingenuousness which was quite unassumed, which explained Lionel's unpopularity with senior clergy, as the cathedral and diocesan staff spoke of themselves.

So here he was running a clothes brush over his one good, ancient suit. Should he walk or should he bike? He preferred bike but had to admit cycle clips did nothing for his trouser turn-ups, which were beginning to fray. He'd walk then. Would it rain again? The dusk was warm enough to suggest thunder. He took his father's umbrella with the monogrammed gold band. 'Style,' said Lionel and twirled it with pleasure.

Towards the end of the street the houses gave up any pretence of respectability. Front doors were painted purple with green banding or had serpents in fluorescent colours squirming up the jambs. There were cars which lacked wheels parked on the weedy gravel of the narrow front gardens. 'Communities,' said Lionel to himself, 'do they exist? Which is mine? Here? The cathedral? Is it place or is it people? Or is it work?' He thought of the messes, the common rooms, the clubs which he had inhabited in his long working life (he did not dignify so random a progression with the description 'career'). What will happen when I don't work? The thought gave him so much pleasure he started to hum: 'If you want to know who we are, we are gentlemen of Japan. On many a vase and flower, on many a screen and fan . . .'

Then he thought of Mick Lee and stopped. He imagined the van pulled off the bypass behind the council house which tonight would have no returning owner. How would his community, his family, cope? In Lionel's experience when some great rent in the fabric occurs, some undeserved misfortune falls, people looked for someone, something, to blame. No one any longer accepts accidents as accidents. The notion of an act of God has disappeared along with belief in God. If there was no God to blame or bow to what could human beings do? They could sue. And doubtless that was what the Lees would do. Who and how much, Lionel wondered as he cleared the terrace, hit the traffic as though it were a bombardment, sprinted across the worn greensward and began to climb the seventy-four steps of the cathedral mound.

* * *

Theodora gazed at her hostess with respect.

'Dovetailing,' said Susan Tye, 'is the most difficult but the most rewarding.' She mumbled a bit because she had tacks in her mouth.

'I didn't remember,' Theodora was diffident, 'I didn't know you had woodwork as a hobby.'

Susan Tye, small with fair hair stretched back from her brow so tightly it seemed to elongate her eyes, snorted.

'Hobby! Needs must when the devil drives. When we came here neither Reggie nor I had a stick. We had to start from scratch.' She ended with pride and indicated what Theodora had classed as a morning room. There was a sparse number of books, some of them on shelves. The shelves were planks of builders' pine, unpainted, and one tier was separated from another by bricks.

Theodora remembered Susan at school. She had been undistinguished except for her concentration on netball where she had compensated for short stature by sharp, painful elbows. Her present expertise seemed a perfectly natural continuation of her younger gifts.

As soon as Theodora had arrived Susan had taken her on a tour of the house. Theodora wasn't sure why. It was as though Susan wished her to be under no illusions, as though she wanted nothing to be hidden from her guest, to get straight how it was she and Reggie lived. But there was apparently nothing to hide. They possessed very little. So, Theodora began to wonder, why the strain? Susan's insistent openness made Theodora feel all the time there was something lurking in one or other of the corners which would come out the moment they had closed the door behind them.

About the house, however, an hour later Theodora had no misapprehensions. It was, apart from its sparsely furnished interior, exactly what you would expect a provost's lodgings to be in such a cathedral close. It was a solid, domestic offspring of the cathedral. It had the same brick, the same capaciousness. It would have suited a provost with a large family, domestic servants and a private income.

‘We rattle around a bit,’ Susan had said. And they did. Room after room had a single piece of furniture in it, a token to claim ownership, as though habitation would follow at some future date. Many of the pieces were incongruous. A dumb waiter stood alone, unsupported by any other piece which might entitle the room to claim the status of what it must have been intended to be, a bedroom. Some of the pieces were in the process of being seen to by Susan’s ministration. Hammers, nails, glue, clamps, bits of veneers, teach yourself carpentry manuals lay at the feet of tables or littered chair seats. As they moved from room to room an undersized springer followed them round greeting each new room as though he’d never seen it before, pushing his nose across the scanty rugs and exploring dusty corners in hope.

‘How long have you been here?’ Theodora enquired.

‘Just moved in, really. Three years this June.’

‘And you were in Brentford before that?’

‘Right. Reggie was the chaplain of the health trust and did a bit for the Midland Theological Institute.’

‘Has he had a parish?’ Theodora, a parish curate, felt nothing else quite counted in the vocated life.

‘Not as such, not, that is to say, a living of his own,’ Susan Tye admitted cautiously. ‘He had an NSM curacy in one of the City churches.’

Theodora knew about City parishes: weekday lunchtime trade and nothing on Sunday. It was a perfectly respectable and very necessary ministry but somehow not quite enough. A ministry built round sandwiches, as it were, suggested the temporary and unstable, a bit like his wife’s domestic arrangements.

Theodora wondered, not for the first time, why she had come, as they clumped up the stairs, the banisters half stripped of paint, the drugget on the floor tacked down on some steps but not on others. Would curiosity about place, about relationship be enough to sustain her through five or six days? Well, time would tell and Susan’s phone call with which she had followed up her letter of invitation haunted her. 'I need someone I can trust but quite outside our narrow little world,' she had said. There was something amiss. But then, Theodora thought, she was rarely asked anywhere where that was not the case.

'Come and see your room,' Susan said. 'We're doing the house up a room at a time, or rather I am,' she said with modest pride. Theodora wondered which rooms had been done. She hadn't met any of those yet.

'This is your room,' said her hostess. 'You'll want to have a wash before supper. There'll be one or two others dropping by. But don't change.' She regarded Theodora's brown suiting. 'Come down when you're ready. There'll be drinks in the kitchen. We'll talk later.'

Well, I suppose that's what I've come for, after all, Theodora thought.

When Theodora looked about her, there was indeed a washstand in the room. A splendid stand, the age of the house, in mahogany with a willow pattern basin and ewer, stood in one corner. It was more difficult to discover a bed. The only other furniture in the room was a chest-like object with no drawers and brass handles on each side of its front. A moment's reflection and the memory of her grandmother's servants' rooms led her to seize the two brass handles, jerk and walk backwards. The truckle bed followed her obediently across the bare boards. Tucked into the space in the upper part of the case were a couple of horse blankets and a coverlet made of the sort of knitted woollen squares which had been destined for refugees in the 1950s.

It all fitted the ethos of the place. The water in the ewer smelt faintly of weed so Theodora left it alone. There seemed to be no point in unpacking given there was nothing to unpack into. So she didn't. There was something to be said for the simple life. Instead she dug her mobile phone out of her bag and dialled the familiar number.

'Betterhouse Vicarage. Geoffrey Brighouse, vicar, here.'

'Safely stowed,' said Theodora as she had promised.

'What's it like?'

'It's a sort of clerical Cold Comfort Farm.'
'Sounds jolly.'
'We shall see.' Theodora was cautious.
'Make the best.' Geoffrey was bracing.
'Of course.' Didn't she always?
'God bless.'
'Thanks. 'Bye.'

CHAPTER FOUR: ENTERTAINING

'Gratitude is so exhausting,' said Susan Tye.

Theodora wondered if she was being rebuked for some lack of it. She contemplated the minute glass of sweet, warm sherry which she'd been offered and, in the absence of anything else forthcoming, taken.

'I mean, everyone seemed to think Reggie should be grateful when he was made Provost. I tell them, they ought to be jolly glad to get him.'

'Was he much sought after?'

Theodora looked at Lionel but his face was as bland as his tone.

'He's a man of wide experience.' Reggie's loyal wife tossed something white and amoeba-like into the sort of pan used by troops in camps in the First World War. It was semicircular and might, Theodora judged, be difficult to balance on the ring of the huge gas range. It was also rather small for feeding what could not be fewer than four and might be more people.

Susan stood at the range adding more salt than Theodora judged wise for any dish. They were gathered in the one fully furnished room in the house. Indeed not only was it fitted out like a kitchen with deal table and bentwood chairs but it appeared to be a furniture store for the rest of the house. To lay the table Susan had urged Theodora to forge a path to dressers ranged round the room through piles of tea chests and bed ends. A life in waiting, Theodora had thought, but waiting for what?

What experience would that be, Theodora wondered. Lionel has come for the sport, not, to be sure, for the home comforts.

'He has the most beautiful handwriting, an absolutely marvellous copperplate,' Susan said.

Theodora thought of all the occasions in modern Church life when that would be an asset.

'And in social skills alone he's light years ahead of the rest of the Chapter.'

Without being blatantly rude, it's going to be difficult to cap that, Theodora thought. But she'd reckoned without Lionel's years of clergy-baiting.

'It's a high standard in the clergy,' Lionel said.

'Tact,' said his hostess heavily, 'takes its toll.'

'He finds his duties as Provost onerous?' Lionel was propped against a spare piece of dresser. He looked spry and alert. Theodora could not make out whether he was raffish or distinguished. He wore a soft brownish greyish tweed suit which fitted just as it should but she noticed it was fraying at the turn-ups.

'Well, no chapter is easy, is it?' Susan Tye poured the salt water into the other half of the semicircular pan and dropped what Theodora feared were lumps of soya into it. Theodora took it as a bad sign that the springer, curled up on an old pair of curtains in the corner, evinced no interest in the cooking.

'You mean the fact that none of them had to apply for their jobs, none of them has to demonstrate that they have any relevant skills for them, and it's no one's business to see that they do anything at all, is bound to end up with people of . . .' Lionel paused and for a moment Theodora thought he was going to say 'indifferent talents', but he drew back.

'Varied or perhaps even ill-matched abilities.' Theodora thought she hadn't heard so comprehensive an indictment of clerical recruitment systems before.

'Absolutely.' Susan's unvarying earnestness carried them all along.

Theodora could not help but admire Susan. Perhaps she had seen in Reggie scope for her talent. Her victory would be to ignore, circumvent or prevent Reggie's incompetence. This, Theodora recognized, was not a foolish or vicious use of talent. Reggie would be better because of Susan. To resolve to make a success of such an unpromising marriage was surely noble. The only reservation Theodora had was that it seemed to depend for its effectiveness on Susan's closing her eyes tight to Reggie's inadequacies: could such a wilful overlooking of the truth be a sure foundation for success?

'Money,' Theodora sought to steer things away from the personal, 'is often a cause of strain in any cathedral chapter.'

Susan stirred the brew in the pan as though it were the rarest of sauces. 'Could you put the bread out?' She motioned to the large sliced white on the dresser before replying. Then she said, 'It's the whole focus of the cathedral's energies at the moment. Reggie spends hours thinking of nothing else. I sometimes fear it's undermining his health.'

There was a noise in the hall as of someone falling over things. A moment later there was the sound of scrabbling as the Provost searched for the door handle, then, after a short delay, Reggie Tye walked in. There was a faint smell of camphor. He gazed with incredulity at his wife and her guests as though these were the last people he'd expected to find in his kitchen.

'Reggie, love.' His wife embraced him, daringly leaving the pans balanced together on the stove. 'You haven't met my old chum, Theo Braithwaite.'

The Provost summoned some of his bruited social skills for the occasion. 'How very nice,' he murmured. 'I think I once met your husband at a CMS conference in Folkestone, many years ago.'

'No,' said Theodora firmly. 'No, I really don't think you can have. I am not married. Possibly my father, Nicholas Braithwaite.'

Reggie seemed to switch gear. 'Nicholas Braithwaite. Oh, yes. Oh, dear me, yes. I'm so sorry. I didn't realize. A great, a most outstanding talent. I hope he is well?'

'He died three years ago.' Theodora hated to disoblige a second time but could hardly do otherwise.

'I'm so very sorry. Are you . . . ?' He hesitated.

Theodora understood him perfectly. 'I'm in deacon's orders. I serve as curate in a parish in south London.'

Theodora could see that Reggie Tye was faced with a dilemma. Nicholas Braithwaite's daughter deserved honour. They were an Anglican family, the Braithwaites, a long line of bishops and deans, chaplains to this and that stretching back, if he mistook him not, to the seventeenth century. On the other hand a mere deacon and a curate warranted nothing more than patronage and contempt. Theodora watched him struggle, interested to see which would win. He was saved by disaster.

The pans, precariously propped against each other, thrown out of balance by some expansion of metal, tottered and fell, one into and one away from the stove. Lionel sprang back to avoid the contents but Reggie was not so nimble. The soya and pasta mix slid down his clerical black.

'Oh darling, do be careful,' said his wife reproachfully. She took a long spoon and retrieved at least some of the mixture as though he might be keeping too large a share for himself. Then she sponged him down and pushed him into a chair at the head of the table. 'Come and say grace before worse befalls.'

Reggie protested, but feebly. 'I thought you said Marcus More was coming.'

'I told you to ask him. Did you?'

'I'm not sure,' the unfortunate Provost admitted. 'I did remember to ask Lionel though,' he said proudly.

Lionel thought of the two million Reggie was supposed to be raising and the cathedral he was supposed to be running as a beacon light of the Church's mission in this diocese, and despaired.

'Never mind, more for us,' said Susan. She placed the tureen of reconstituted goodies on the table, shuffled four cold plates in front of Reggie, folded her hands and gazed expectantly at her husband.

'Benedictus benedicat,' coughed the Provost rapidly and they fell to. For a moment or two they ate in silence. Lionel meticulously took small pieces of clerical black fluff from his mouth and placed them on the edge of his plate. Theodora, who had a long day, hoped bread would be offered but it wasn't. Not many of the soya lumps seemed to have survived contact with Reggie's waistcoat.

The springer made a brief unhopeful round of the diners and then mewed at the French windows. Susan let him out. 'He's a bit of a beggar, actually,' she said with pride. 'Since we went vegetarian, he's started going across the close to Bishop Dick's. They're big meat-eaters and of course they do have to do a lot of entertaining.'

Theodora wondered if she might get a chance to follow the springer later in the evening.

'I thought the Bishop was away,' said Lionel who had finished and hence was able to turn his attention to conversation.

'He's in Jedda at the moment,' Susan answered, as though this absence were a matter of pride which reflected well on them all.

'No, that was last week,' said the Provost. 'This week he's in Los Angeles.'

'Still, they keep a big household,' Susan pursued. 'They have a fulltime cook.'

'Do you ever dine there?' It was Lionel at his old tricks, Theodora thought.

'He doesn't waste his hospitality on his own clergy,' said the Provost bitterly.

Theodora wondered whose decision it had been that the Tyes should 'go vegetarian'.

'How's your brother?' asked the Provost suddenly, turning to Lionel. Theodora was disconcerted to see Lionel flush deeply.

'He's as well as can be expected.'

'Wretched business,' said Reggie. 'Daily in our prayers,' he added.

Lionel murmured something inarticulate which might have been thanks.

'Lionel's brother is in prison for drunken driving,' said Susan Tye chattily across Lionel and addressing Theodora. She clearly belonged to the 'Christian brotherhood equals total truthfulness' brigade. For once Theodora could think of no possible response to this.

Susan collected the plates as though taking in exercise books, and produced a bowl of good-looking Coxes and something with a thick red plastic rind on it. Reggie fell on the provender hungrily. Theodora and Lionel followed. Susan looked disapproving at such reckless indulgence of sensuous desire.

When they could in decency eat no more, Susan Tye said, 'Now, Reggie, you and Lionel will want to talk shop. Theo and I have some gossip to catch up on.'

Theodora wondered whether the significant events of paths which had not crossed for ten years could count as gossip. Surely they ought to value their own and each other's lives more highly than that. Also, why shouldn't Reggie and Lionel help with the washing-up? These tail-ends of rituals belonging to another way of life were tiresome.

A poor cook Susan Tye might have been but she was an efficient or anyway fast washer-up. When Reggie had shuffled out clutching his cup of Nescafé and limping ahead of Lionel, she sluiced the plates rapidly under the cold tap before wiping her hands on the thin towel and planting herself at the table.

'I expect you thought it was odd me asking you down after all this time.'

'Well, it's always good to see old friends.' Theodora was cautious.

'The point is, I need someone to act on our behalf.'

'Act, on whose behalf?'

'Ours, mine and Reggie's.'

'What sort of act?'

'Reggie's being blackmailed.'

If Susan had wanted an effect she had it. Theodora was perfectly used to people confiding in her. She never invited confidences but a large number of people felt, mistakenly in Theodora's own opinion, that they could trust her; that she was sane, balanced and discreet. At this moment, however, she had to prevent herself asking what on earth Reggie could have done that anyone would care about. Instead she asked, 'Who's the blackmailer and for what?'

'That's what I want you to find out.'

'Why me?'

'You've done one or two things like that before, haven't you?'

'More or less by accident.'

'That was what your vicar said. But still, accident or no, you know the ropes.'

Theodora was nonplussed. How dare Susan Tye get in touch with Geoffrey and what had the man said and why had he not warned her? 'Why not ask the police?'

'There are things you can't tell the police. If that weren't so there could be no possibility of blackmail.' Susan was logical. She had a point. 'As to who is doing it or for what purpose, I don't know the answer to either question.'

'How do you know he's being blackmailed?'

'I saw his Post Office savings book.'

'Good heavens, I thought they'd discontinued those years ago.'

'Reggie keeps to some old-fashioned ways,' Susan Tye said with dignity. 'He's taken out four thousand pounds over the last four months.'

'But how do you know he's paying blackmail? He might be giving the money to charity or spending it legitimately.'

'You don't know Reggie.'

This was true but Theodora wasn't sure she wanted to fill that lacuna. 'And he's worried. He's not well,' Susan hurried on. 'At times he's furtive.'

'How does it show?' Theodora was genuinely interested to know how the shambling, clumsy, slow man could do anything which would escape notice.

'He goes off to make phone calls from public phone boxes. He looks guilty.'

'What on earth could he be guilty of?' Theodora felt hysterical. She found Susan's intense, dramatic manner hard to cope with. Her instinct was to reject any attempt to draw her into this tornado of emotions. Why should I feel what she wants me to feel? It's just a species of bullying.

Susan leaned forward. 'Before I married Reggie, I realized that he might have a past.'

Oh, come off it, Theodora did not say. He's a cathedral provost. That's a guarantee that he has done, thought, felt, experienced nothing of the least interest or importance for the entirety of his manhood.

'What I want to know is not so much "what" as "who"? I can't bear to think of someone making life hell for poor Reggie.'

Theodora felt the destructive pity welling up in her for her old school friend. That's always the way I'm got at, she thought resentfully. She hadn't reflected on the reasons why a sensible woman of thirty should marry a hopeless, unattractive man twenty-five years her senior. Now she could see why. If you couldn't have children then perhaps mothering a hopeless case like Reggie Tye was the next best thing.

'You know,' Susan was continuing, 'he has climbed the ladder of success and there are those who would bring him down.'

Theodora thought this was an unfortunate metaphor in the circumstances. But Susan pressed on regardless. 'And he's such a dear. He couldn't harm a fly.'

'In that case he'll be difficult to blackmail,' Theodora pointed out.

Susan paused to reflect. 'Well, you can't ever be absolutely sure about anyone. He might have made mistakes, slips which he wouldn't want known. What would be a mere peccadillo for any other man might reflect badly in the case of one of the senior clergy. They have to set such a high standard and be above reproach, you know.'

The condescension set Theodora's teeth on edge. Susan didn't notice her audience but continued to dramatize. 'I'm sure he's not done anything really dishonest. But success attracts envy.'

Theodora marvelled that Susan could think being the provost of a cathedral counted as being successful. They didn't come dimmer, in Theodora's view. But then, she thought, I can't carp since it's not something I've ever aimed at. Progress in prayer, improvement in moral sensitivity, control of impulse, these were Theodora's criteria. Her friends reckoned she was not without her own obtuseness.

'I so hoped you'd be able to help me. I don't know anyone else I'd remotely trust who has the right experience.' Susan was suddenly helpless.

Hell's teeth, Theodora thought. 'Inquiries of the sort you'd need to make would take time and I really can't stay longer than the week. I must be back in the parish by next Friday lunchtime.' Set against her friend's distress it sounded frail, indeed heartless.

'I had hoped you might stretch it a few days more.' Susan had clearly scented her weakening. 'We've got quite a social round here and there's the cathedral. You like cathedrals, don't you?' She sounded as though she was verifying her guest's taste in eggs. 'If you could just get me a clue or a lead of some kind, I'm sure I could go on from there myself.'

'The most I could promise is to keep my eyes and ears open while I'm here and see if I can pick up anything.'

Susan's small intense face with its excess of concentration cleared into a smile. She looked almost pretty.

'Fill me in about who he works with and so on. We may as well start with those who know him best and have best access to his character and background.'

'He works with Archdeacon More, the diocesan secretary. He's a scholar and rather a pain. A lot of negative attitudes. Doesn't want anything to happen. Costive. My counselling course said he'd be the character type to try and manipulate. Though, of course, that doesn't make him a blackmailer. He hasn't made a success of family life. The daughter ran off with a Greek waiter and the boy, he's a couple of years younger, keeps getting run in for driving cars without letting their owners know. The only thing he wants is a car and somewhere else to live apart from the family home.'

'He finds his father dominating?' Theodora hazarded.

'Oh, yes. Marcus likes to be top dog. But having heaved himself up there, he doesn't seem to know what to do with it. Lionel says he doesn't have any plans or anything. Lionel says sustaining the position, coming down hard on people who threaten it, is all he's good at.'

Theodora thought she'd met several in the Church who carried on like that.

'He's been in post a long time,' Susan concluded. 'I should think he knows what's going on just by having a finger in so many pies.'

'Who else?'

'Well, Lionel, of course. But I rather like Lionel. I wouldn't want it to be him.'

Theodora was glad of that. She quite liked Lionel herself, though she saw he wasn't enamoured of the clergy — or, anyway, the senior clergy.

'He has shady connections though.' Susan was entering into the spirit of the thing. 'His brother is in prison.'

'I gathered. What for?'

'It was all a bit of a shame. Vincent, the brother, was an architect with a small practice in Gainshurst. He was coming home from a meeting one nasty February night last year through Cray Martyr and his car was surrounded by louts loosing from the pub. He had a choice to drive on through the crowd or to stop and be mugged. So he drove on and one of them landed up on his bonnet. The man was drunk but so, the police said, was Vincent. Or, anyway, over the limit, so they put him away for three years. It's devastated Lionel more than Vincent, I think. Lionel is rather pukka. Ex-infantry. The family had land in Dorset. Gentlemen, if you see what I mean.'

Theodora saw. 'How long has Vincent got to go?'

'Another two years, I think.'

'It hardly makes Lionel a blackmailer.'

'No,' Susan admitted, 'no, it doesn't, does it?'

Theodora thought, why am I being drawn into this? This is an innocent, ordinary, indeed dull society. What evidence have I, apart from the intensity of Susan's emotion, that Reggie is being blackmailed? 'Who else does he work with?'

'There's Kate Wale. Canon Wale. She has to work closely with Reggie and with Marcus More, especially over the appeal.'

'Which appeal would that be?'

'The cathedral's falling down. Reggie is spearheading the restoration fund.'

Theodora thought 'spearheading' sounded rather energetic for the sort of thing Reggie could be imagined doing. 'How much do you need?'

'Over two million. But Reggie says English Heritage are going to give the first quarter-million. Then we're on our own.'

'I suppose it's worth it?' Theodora's mind wandered to the glimpses of the building she'd had on the journey in and then from her bedroom window.

'When you see round it, you'll see how very important it is to keep it up.' Susan was didactic.

Damn it, Theodora thought, who's the pro round here, her or me? Susan had shown few signs of being interested in Christianity other than in its purely social and conventional aspect at either school or university. Since marrying into it, however, she seemed to have taken over the entire stock of received ideas uncritically. Theodora tried to recall what she knew of Susan's people. She seemed to remember a father who had collected his daughter at holiday times, a civil servant with frequent postings abroad. Cheltenham had many such daughters. Her mother had been rather like Susan, intense, worried, hyperactive.

'So would Kate Wale as a colleague want to squeeze a few thousand out of Reggie?'

'She's rich. She married some property dealer type, Leslie, who works out of Docklands. It wouldn't be the money. It might not be the money with any of them. I mean Reggie is suffering. That might be the point, mightn't it? Someone might just want to hurt him regardless of the money. Make him sweat.'

'Would Kate Wale want to do that?'

'She always seems pleasant enough. Rather kind of condescending but not really mean. But how can one tell for certain?'

'I must say I can't see how I can—' Theodora began, but Susan cut her off.

'I've got it all worked out. You see, he does it on the first Saturday of each month.'

'Does what?'

'Draws money from the post office. It's the first of October tomorrow, Saturday,' she added in case Theodora had forgotten. 'I thought if you followed him and saw where he left it, who he paid it to, we could . . .'

'We could what?' Theodora asked, genuinely curious.

'Well, I haven't actually worked out what we could do next. But it would be a step forward, wouldn't it? I mean if he made a drop somewhere.'

Theodora thought, she's been reading too much police fiction. However, she was clearly expected to fall in with this. 'Does Reggie get any sort of signal, a letter or a phone call, to trigger the withdrawals?'

'Not here, he doesn't. But he might at the office. But I rather think not, unless it's coded.' Susan seemed to come upon this thought for the first time. It excited her. 'He couldn't get it *en clair* because his secretary opens his mail and the phones are the switchboard variety and I know they listen in.'

'What time of day does he make the withdrawal?'

'Ten in the morning from the Silver Street branch just below Sainsbury's in the high street. It's ten minutes' walk from here.'

'Why haven't you followed him yourself?'

'Oh, I've tried but it's quite difficult with one's own husband. Last month he turned round just as I came round the corner, so of course I had to wave and move on. The time before that I lost him after he'd made the withdrawal. You see,' Susan was earnest, 'I haven't your experience, your talents.'

Theodora weighed this one up. 'What exactly would that experience be?' Damn it, she was a curate in a Church of England parish, not a gumshoe.

'Geoffrey said you were extremely efficient.'

'That's as his curate, not as a . . .' Theodora strove for words, 'a private eye.'

Susan giggled. 'That's just what I'm asking for, isn't it? I want you to eye up Reggie privately, or anyway without giving the game away. You will do it, though, won't you? I really can't stand the idea of Reggie being sucked dry or being hurt. You don't know what it's like when you're married to someone.'

Theodora admitted she didn't and the thought of Reggie made her glad about that. She felt Susan's motherly instincts had clouded her reason in the case of Reggie.

'All right,' she said at last. 'I'll shadow Reggie, if I can, and see what he does with the money. It may be something quite innocent, you know.'

'But why should he hide his Post Office savings book in his collar box, if it is all quite innocent?'

Theodora thought, I bet only the clergy have collar boxes nowadays with the death of the detachable collar. And a glance at Reggie would make it not so unlikely that he would see a collar box as an absolutely private, and therefore perfectly appropriate, place to file correspondence in. 'Where does he keep his chequebook?' she asked, just to test.

'In the top right-hand drawer of his desk,' Susan answered promptly. So that was right.

Susan sat back in her chair with the air of having accomplished a supreme mission. 'I knew I could rely on you. I knew you'd—'

There was the sound of a telephone ringing near at hand and being answered; the murmur of voices and then a scrabbling at the door and Reggie's soft fleshy face shining pale in the light from the passage behind him. Was it Theodora's imagination or was there sweat on his brow? Behind him, Theodora glimpsed Lionel, his face shadowed and unreadable.

'It's the police,' Reggie said. 'They want to come round and have a word about Mick Lee. The man killed this afternoon.'

'Right,' said Susan, relaxed and restored now that her own problem was taken care of. 'I'll get some more coffee going.'

'It's not what you think,' said Lionel, his voice distant and constrained. 'It's worse than you think. It wasn't an accident. The police are saying Lee was killed intentionally. Murdered, in fact.'

* * *

Kate Wale looked at Leslie. 'Yes. He was one of ours,' said her husband.

'Did you know when you took him on?'

'I can't vet every brickie a subsidiary company hires.' Leslie's long bony face was turned away from her. The light in Kate's lounge left big shadows over the deep chairs. Leslie lay rather than sat, seemingly on the edge of complete exhaustion. He was thin and muscular. He wore a dark blue, three-piece City suit and a lilac pink shirt which was fashionable at the time with his kind. Kate recognized it as a uniform. The difficulty with wearing a uniform, she thought, was that it made people who recognized it as such wonder of a person what non-uniform would be for them. She had a vision of Leslie in denims and T-shirt. But no, he wasn't like that anymore. He'd come a long way from the Cray Martyr style of dressing.

Leslie uncoiled his hands from the whisky glass and placed it on a tiny table at his side. Automatically Kate rose and slipped a little cork mat under it. Leslie thought how endearing he'd found Kate's genteel ways when they had first married. But just recently, as the strains of work mounted, he had a desire to throw his clothes on the floor, leave papers strewn over the table, pile plates on chairs. He realized the place never smelt of anything. He wanted ardently to be what Kate had in mind they both should be: rich, successful, insulated. He'd been as eager as she to leave Cray Martyr behind. He rarely went back, if he could help it, preferring to use agents and middlemen instead. But his work, unlike hers, kept him dealing with the people of his youth. You can't have it both ways, he reflected; his success as a developer and builder grew out of knowing how Cray Martyr men thought and worked. Only now he felt it might not be enough to keep the Lees at bay.

'How could you . . . ?' Kate couldn't think of a phrase which would cover Leslie's activities. Leslie did not answer. Kate tried another tack.

'How long have you . . . we . . .' Kate was loyal; she associated herself, as far as she was allowed, with Leslie's work, 'had him, had Mick Lee?'

'We've only just got in on the Giltchrist thing. We took an interest in Elvestone's a year ago when they were going down.'

'It's a long time since the other thing,' Kate said.

Leslie knew what she meant. 'I wasn't responsible for the road plan. And anyway, it never came to anything.'

'But the Lees saw it as a threat. You made enemies of them.'

'Price of success.' Leslie smiled briefly. 'Anyway, they can't blame me for Mick Lee's death. There's absolutely no connection between us.'

Kate tried to read the expression in his voice and could not. 'I thought you said it was an accident.' She was alert to his every implication.

'Lees don't have accidents.'

Kate wondered what he meant, whether she believed him. She looked at him helplessly. She wanted him to go to the office every day and return at seven, to read *The Times* and play golf on Saturdays. She knew very well this wasn't a heroic aspiration but it was hers. She didn't want anyone to undermine that prospect. To keep it, in fact, she'd take measures herself.

'You know what the Lees are,' Leslie said. It was almost as though he were taunting her, making it worse, failing to contribute to her pokerwork comfort.

Kate knew. Hadn't she, like Leslie, grown up in Cray Martyr? She remembered old Mr Lee, Mick's father, who had no teeth and an earring in his ear long before it was fashionable for men to do so. She knew the Lee brothers, close in age and close to her and Leslie's age. The Lees had never, like more normal youths, clung to lamp-posts and destroyed corporation benches. More normal youths, their limbs as uncoordinated and knotted as young trees, had hung about the crossroads joking mindlessly with each other, nervously lascivious with any girl who entrusted herself to the group. But the Lees had not been part of that culture. No, the Lees always had purposes, enterprises on hand. They first accompanied, then drove, well under age, without a licence between them, lorries with grabs on their backs, or huge Fords. Kate remembered a picture she retained from those days of one such vehicle lurching round the corner, tipping over to one side, brown tattooed limbs, mostly arms but some legs too, dangling and nodding out of all four open windows. It had remained with her as a symbol of anarchy, of the alienness of the Lees.

Surely Leslie wasn't going to have to deal, and deal from an inferior position, with that clan again? What had they worked for if not to elevate themselves from such needs?

'You weren't to blame,' she said. 'You didn't even know.'

He shook his head. 'They'll know. They'll find out. They aren't reasonable people.'

The mobile phone ringing on the table between them was almost a relief. Leslie reached for it and listened before he said, 'What, now? Are you sure?'

When the caller had rung off he held the instrument for a moment as though dazed. Finally he folded it into its neat case before looking at Kate. 'The police want to talk to me about Lee's death. They're saying it wasn't an accident.'

CHAPTER FIVE: FOLLOWING

'And keep from us all perils and dangers of this night that awake we may watch with Christ and asleep we may rest in Him.' Theodora concluded her prayers and sat back on the truckle bed to review the day. She felt too much had happened. It was indecent to cram so much experience into one diurnal round.

She had pushed the bed up under the window. Then she banged both sides of the casement with an accurate shoe and managed to get it open and let some air into the stuffy room. She looked out on to the darkened close. The cathedral spire rose from its cradle of scaffold. There was no moon, and stars could no longer be seen over the lights of the city.

She had looked forward to a quiet week catching up with an old friend and exploring a cathedral she didn't know. Now blackmail and murder had slipped in from the wings to spoil it all. The police had come soon after Reggie had broken the news to them. They had come in the form of an inspector and a sergeant, scarcely glimpsed by the women. She had caught sight of two solid men with low persistent voices as they moved down the hall to be closeted with Reggie and Lionel in Reggie's study. They hadn't wanted, naturally, to see Theodora or Susan. The women made more coffee in the kitchen and waited.

When the kitchen door opened again and Reggie squeezed through he looked as though he might burst into tears. It was Lionel who gave them the news.

'They say it's murder because they've examined the scaffolding and found that the plank Lee trod on his way down had been sawn nearly through very recently.'

'I have to say I find that very difficult to believe.' The Provost put in his contribution. He was used to saying things in a decisive voice and having people believe him. It irked him that his one talent had left the police unmoved. 'I told them . . .' He trailed off. Just for a moment Theodora caught a glimpse of a world which would not be told anything by the Church, where the Church as a pronouncer on worldly matters was not thought to be reliable, was not informed, had not understood the questions and hence was doomed to be ignored.

Lionel went on. 'They're trying to find out whether the plank was deliberately tampered with or whether it was faulty when it went up. These particular planks were new into the depot on Tuesday and were brought down here on Thursday evening. They need to know who put them up and when.'

He's orderly, Theodora thought. Is it his military training or some other sort? He doesn't buttress his ego either. He'd just like the facts to be laid bare and something sensible done, not counting the cost.

'What the police really need to know,' Lionel was pressing on, 'is who had access to the site on Thursday evening.'

'That's ridiculous,' Susan Tye said. 'Hundreds of people walk past the cathedral. Reggie takes the dog out on Thursday evenings. The vergers are always in and out. Someone would see anyone who was going for the planks at an unorthodox hour.'

'It would have to be after dark,' Lionel pointed out.

'Yes, well, they'll have a lot of checking to do, is all I can say.' Susan sounded aggrieved.

'Of course,' the Provost broke in, 'it will all be the responsibility of the contractors. I forget their name but clearly it's up to them.'

'No one is suggesting the Chapter caused the man's death,' said Lionel, 'but we ought perhaps to have taken a bit more interest in what was going on. I gather that the original firm, Elvestone's, was taken over just before they started work here. In fact, the police say that Elvestone's were taken over by Wale Holdings.'

'Kate's husband?' Susan asked.

'Yes.'

'How awful for Kate.'

'And rather more so for Leslie.'

'It's not their fault,' Susan protested. 'He couldn't be expected to know everything that goes on all his building sites, could he?'

'Would Leslie have known the Lees?' Lionel was clearly pursuing his own line of inquiry.

'I shouldn't have thought so,' Susan said. 'Not on Kate's visiting list, anyhow. Just the sort Kate and Leslie have left behind.'

'You can never leave the Lees behind,' Lionel said. 'The Lees are life.'

Susan stared at him with sudden intelligence. 'Are they the same family your brother killed one of?'

Lionel nodded. 'Vincent killed the youngest, Jon. Mick was the middle one and there's one still alive, called Deke.'

'I can't see why we should be held responsible for all this.' Reggie was several moves behind the rest of the conversation. 'What do we have a comptroller for?'

'He's been off sick for nine months with DTs,' Lionel pointed out. 'We ought to have kept an eye. We're quick enough to tell the rest of the world how it should manage its business in a just society.' Lionel thought of Vincent. His tone was bitter. 'We don't begin to set an example.'

'That's outrageous,' said the Provost.

'If that's so, then we should shut up prattling about social justice,' said Lionel.

Theodora thought this was quite brave. Then she remembered that Lionel was within striking distance of retiring.

'If the plank was tampered with,' said Susan to keep the peace and protect her husband, 'what's the motive? Who would want to kill Mick Lee and why?'

There was silence. Theodora watched the contestants. The Provost set his weak man's jaw in a pout. Lionel fixed his eye on Susan. 'With the Lees it could be someone with a score to settle. The Lees are not a popular family. They've run Cray Martyr for years like their own personal fiefdom. Or, and this is what the police are suggesting, it could be that there was another motive.'

'Go on,' Susan prompted.

'Mick Lee's recently been spending a lot. New car and so on. The police seemed to feel he might have access to more money than he was earning.'

Susan wouldn't say it so Theodora did. 'Blackmail.'

'The inspector didn't say that,' the Provost broke in.

'No,' Lionel agreed, 'he didn't. He left us to take the inference.'

'I think you're reading a lot into what he said,' said Reggie Tye.

'I've known Inspector Spurt for several years.' Lionel was complacent. 'Actually, he was my sergeant in Cyprus. He's not quick but he is thorough and reliable and honest. Admirable qualities in people in posts of responsibility.' Lionel switched his gaze back to Reggie.

The Provost said, 'I didn't know you were in the forces.'

'No, well, you wouldn't, would you? I've only been in post ten years.' His tone implied that the Provost had the retentive memory of a fruit fly. 'But I was.'

Susan reckoned this was enough. 'What about a nightcap and then call it a day?'

Theodora surveyed her host and hostess. She'd no wish to watch their discomfiture. 'I've had a long day. I wonder if you'd mind if I went up?'

So here she was gazing at the cathedral and wondering what had happened there this afternoon when a man had stumbled to his death. Would someone from the cathedral take on the Lee family as a pastoral concern? Or would they do as the world would and shrug it off on to someone else? She thought about the three very different societies of Giltchrist, Cray Martyr and Gainshurst. How did they relate to each other? Giltchrist seemed cut off on a hill with a quite different perspective on human life. She recalled the journey with Lionel, first the artisans' cottages and travellers' vans of Cray Martyr, then the fat leafy pastures of Gainshurst; finally, the solid Edwardian clerical houses of Giltchrist's close.

Had Reggie Tye been blackmailed by Mick Lee and, if so, on what grounds? And had the Provost then taken a saw and prepared the way for the demise of Lee? Surely not. It seemed improbable that Reggie could hold a saw straight long enough to make any impression on a plank. Then Theodora's mind lurched. There was someone in the Tye household who could hold a saw. She dismissed the notion instantly. The thought of either of the Tyes encompassing the death of another person was beyond belief. All the same, she wished she'd been able to be present at the police interview with Reggie and Lionel. What on earth would she do tomorrow shadowing the Provost? Really, what an idiocy! How did she come to be involving herself in this Fred Karno show?

* * *

At a quarter to seven the next morning, Theodora rose and crossed the close to attend the first Eucharist of the day in the cathedral. She gave herself the pleasure of walking round the outside first. The piles of planks, scaffold poles and clamps were stacked carelessly at the foot of the tower. There was no fence round them. Anyone could have got at them. The close was not closed at night but neither was it on the way to anywhere. You'd have had to come specially, with intent.

A flattened bell summoned her across the strip of grass from the Provost's Lodging to the cathedral. The verger wasn't robed but had a large plastic badge on his suit lapel.

It read, 'Harry Seed, Head Verger.' Theodora couldn't see the point of using the word 'verger', which would be obscure to the uninstructed. If they were going to abandon the usual dress, they'd have to abandon the traditional language too. What would you call a verger in modern demotic? An assistant, perhaps. An assistant what and to whom? It wouldn't easily go on a plastic badge.

The entrance in the south wall at the west end stood open. Theodora walked down the nave, allowing the building to work on her. The red brick inside was purplish. The windows in the north and south clerestories eschewed the pictorial or narrative and replaced them with the symbolic. The artist's favourite colours, yellow, red and green, blazed forth with apocalyptic beasts, trees of Jesse, Noah's arks, pillars of fire, ravens, eagles, lions, phoenixes and serpents. The effect was of a bestiary which was in some way threatening. The artist clearly preferred the Old Testament and the Book of Revelation to any more familiar sources. It was a pity too, Theodora reflected, that so many crematoria were built in brick. Giltchrist could not help but remind one of them. Cathedrals, indeed all places of worship, should, of course, remind people of death but in the context of a particular way of living. Not, as here, with threat and menace and strangeness, by references too arcane to be intelligible.

Trained instinct took Theodora to where the Eucharist would be celebrated. The Lady chapel was marked off from the nave by a lattice of bronze spears. Did anyone ever notice how like a prison or a mausoleum such a design was? Wasn't anyone repulsed by it? Or are we all so dead to the look of things that it really doesn't matter what architects do to us? Here a single mind was responsible for all the artefacts and details so that no part of the spectator's experience was unorganized or left to chance. There was no escape; his glass, his pews, his lights, his candlesticks, even his paten and chalice in Arts and Crafts beaten copper. Wherever the eye went it could not escape the architect's vision. That diversity, that eclecticism of object and adjunct which older cathedrals and churches displayed, where generation after generation had been able to branch out and make their own offering according to their own time and predilections, which allowed the worshipper to experience a variety, to be free to choose — that heritage of Anglicanism was, in Giltchrist, not available.

The congregation was Anglican in number and composition. There were three old women, one young girl and an old man. Theodora knelt in the architect-designed pews where it wasn't clear which bits you sat on and which you knelt on. Theodora wondered who would be taking the service. The printed notice on the cathedral door had not been changed from last week so there was no knowing what to expect. Reggie, she knew, was not in residence. She had checked that Canon Wale wasn't; and that left the precentor who was on holiday. So whom had they routed out to stand in? 'Who's celebrating?' she whispered to the verger as he handed her the fat chunk of an ASB.

'Father Angel from Cray Martyr is on the rota. I think he's turned up. He generally does, in the end,' he said ominously.

Theodora was aware of a slight rustle disturbing the deep silence of an ill-attended early Eucharist. The priest appeared like a magician from behind a tiny door to the north of the altar. He was tall with silky pale gold hair slicked back from a prominent brow and nose. He was vested in cassock alb, dalmatic and, my goodness me, maniple. Haven't seen one of those since Great-uncle Theodore last celebrated at St Mary's Bourne Street. As he stepped up to the altar, she saw, peeping from beneath the cassock alb, the gleam of a well-polished brown riding boot. Theodora, inferring that the ASB would not be wanted, put it to one side and prepared to enjoy whatever was offered.

The Reverend Tobias Angel did not disappoint. He sailed swiftly and professionally through a version of the Roman Catholic Mass which predated Vatican Two by some three hundred years. Theodora was interested to notice that all five of the congregation knew exactly where they were and what to do. So Father Tobias had his following. They reached the blessing in twenty-five minutes flat. Anglican it hardly was, but the panache of the celebrant and the fervour of the congregation were cheering. After a decent interval, Theodora edged out of the chapel and made her way past the apocalyptic beasts blazing out from the windows in the strengthening sun to the north door.

Cropping the edge of the grass in a dedicated way was a smart Connemara, dragging behind him a dog cart in freshly varnished oak. His bridle shone, his hooves were oiled, his mane waved becomingly down his neck in a way that reminded Theodora of his master's own hair. Theodora searched her jacket pocket and found the packet of Polos. The horse did not cease to crop the grass but swivelled one ear and then one eye in her direction, just in case.

'Keeping your options open,' she said.

The pony raised his head, inspected her hand, scooped up the Polo and returned instantly to the grass.

'There's not much he won't eat,' said the owner's voice. Theodora turned round to take in the full glory of Tobias Angel in clerical driving gear. He had a long brown driving jacket and fawn cords. The polished brown boots were seen to be topped with brown gaiters. Under the jacket was a fawn linen shirt worn with a clerical collar. Pretty good, Theodora thought, as a combination of modern and nineteenth-century, clerical and horsy.

'I very much enjoyed your Mass. It's nice to hear the old rite,' Theodora said.

'Never bettered,' agreed Angel. 'I don't know what hubris makes us suppose we can improve on it.'

What was the accent, Theodora wondered. Irish, Australian? Only faint but certainly not entirely English. 'Do the Chapter . . . ?' Theodora enquired.

'Loathe it.' Angel was complacent. 'But they're so idle they can't be bothered to do even their own duties so they certainly can't afford to strike anyone off the rota who's willing to turn out. I regard it as a solemn duty to keep the lump of cathedral worship leavened with catholic practice.'

Theodora could see that he did. 'And do you generally drive up?'

'Public transport's so poor and Christopher likes an outing. It's uphill most of the way here so he works up an appetite and, of course, it's downhill back. So it suits him.'

'He's extremely handsome.' Theodora smelt the mixture of horse sweat, leather and oil and for a moment envied the Reverend Tobias.

'He is generally admired. I'd best be off before the chaps in peaked caps start objecting to his lawn-mowing activities.'

Father Angel dived under the seat of the trap and produced a brown bowler which he clapped on his head. As he turned, the verger, who had oozed out from the north door behind them, cleared his throat. 'Message from the Provost, Father. Would you care to give him a moment of your time? It's about the accident yesterday. One of your parishioners, I believe, a Mr Lee.'

Angel stopped being affable to Theodora and swung round on the verger. 'My compliments to the Provost. Since, however, no one of the Chapter could be bothered to come to the first service of the day, the opus dei, in their own cathedral, I regret my own parish duties prevent my waiting on any of them. If the Provost wants to discuss Mick Lee he can come down and see me. I receive parish visits between five and seven. Tuesday to Friday.'

Theodora found this speech impressive. She could see its justice but wouldn't have been brave enough to deliver it herself.

'Was Mick Lee a churchman?' she asked as Angel swung himself up into the driving seat and took the reins.

'Not as such, but for some reason he had his boy done. Henry. He was sickly at birth and I think they think of baptism as prophylactic.'

'Which in a sense,' Theodora said, 'it is.'

Father Angel brought his eyes down from their resting place between his horse's ears and scrutinized her. 'You know too much theology for a layman.'

Theodora saw that his abrasiveness was not confined to senior clergy. 'I'm in deacon's orders and,' she added quickly, 'intending to stay in them.'

This was the test. There were Anglo-Catholic clergy who denied the validity of priestly orders for women and there were Anglo-Catholic clergy who simply did not care for women as part of the human race. She waited to see which way it would fall.

'Ah, right,' said Father Tobias, giving, Theodora had to admit, nothing away.

'Will you be visiting the family?' Theodora asked.

'Of course. And, if they'll let me, doing the funeral. But we shan't get the body till after the inquest.'

'Which is when?' Theodora thought she might as well know.

'Tuesday.' Father Angel paused and then evidently found Theodora congenial enough to add, 'I gather from the Provost's impertinent invitation that the rumours are correct. There's something odd about the death.'

'I'm staying as the guest of Susan Tye,' Theodora thought it only fair to come clean, 'and, yes, the police saw the Provost last night.'

'What's up?' asked Angel abruptly.

'The plank Mick Lee trod on the way down may not have been sound.' After all this was going to make the local if not the national press in due course. Then she thought, but it's the Provost's blackmailer, if any, I'm supposed to be after. Why am I being drawn into Mick Lee's death? There is no connection, she told herself firmly. Reggie Tye is incapable of murder.

'Of course, Mick Lee isn't a stranger to the Chapter,' Angel said. He tugged at the reins and Christopher reluctantly relinquished his attachment to the lawn and raised his head for the off. 'And you would be?' Angel asked suddenly, looking down on her.

'Braithwaite. Theodora Braithwaite.'

'Braithwaite. Ah, yes. A famous father. Good catholic family. Lots of generations of priests. Pity he didn't have a son.'

And with that he eased the reins and Christopher struck off in a nice brisk march.

* * *

Kate Wale took up the phone and gave it all her attention. The voice was muffled but it was certainly male and demotic.

'Mick Lee got smashed,' it said.

'Who is that?'

'Guess who's going to be dead next.'

'Who are you? I can't hear you.'

'I thought you might like to know, so you can enjoy your weekend. He's smashed. Tell your Leslie: keep off the patch or he's next. Right?'

The phone went click at the other end. Kate put her own instrument down. She was trembling. Clergy do get deranged calls from time to time. She'd been on a course so she knew. She knew there was a code for tracing where a call had originated, only she couldn't remember it. She had just reached for the code book on the rack above her desk when the phone rang again.

'Leslie,' she said with relief. 'Leslie, I've just had a phone call.'

'I'm just leaving the office, sweetheart. I've got a couple of ends to tie up. I won't be back till late.'

'But Leslie, it's Saturday and we need to talk. I tell you I've just had . . .'

'I know, lovie, but this thing's coming to the boil. Got to get it sorted. Be back for supper. Be a good girl.'

Kate didn't have an analytical mind. She hadn't needed one. She reacted to feelings. If anyone had said to her that conversation wasn't a possible one between rational equals she'd not have understood. But she did know that her own needs had been ignored and she was expected to fit in with Leslie's plans and attitudes, while she hadn't been allowed even to state let alone discuss hers. Instinctively she looked for someone with whom she could, as she put it, 'share' her hurt and anger. Only it was Saturday. Sharon from Cray Martyr didn't come in to clean on Saturday.

Her anger subsided to be replaced by fear. The threatening call had achieved its object. For a moment she felt panic. Was it just the call of a druggie or a wino randomly telephoning any number to hand? Or was it deliberately contemplated malice? The man knew about Mick Lee, and he knew Leslie's name. And he'd coupled them together. There was something so graphic about 'smashed'. What was he planning or threatening to do? She picked up the instrument again and dialled Leslie's mobile. The voice sang its refrain, 'The Vodaphone you have called may be switched off. Please try again later.' I mustn't let it stress me, she told herself. Blessed are the pure in heart, she thought, resorting to another diction. And Kate never for a moment doubted that she was pure in heart.

Kate never thought of anything painful for very long. As she'd grown more successful, attained what she called to herself, and sometimes to others too, 'her position', she'd found it easier to impose her own estimate of herself on those around her. Now all she had to do to restore her confidence was to see her own view of herself reflected in other people's eyes. She'd go into the village and shop a bit for the spirituality circle meeting this evening and come back via Andrew Seamley's. He was always good for a laugh and a bit of gossip, him and his old stick-in-the-mud ways.

* * *

Gainshurst on Saturday morning was bright and shining. No litter desecrated its gutters. Its 1930s mock Tudor orderliness reassured. It seemed to validate a social order which had not, in reality, endured from that decade but which had returned. The gap between rich and poor, the need, and meeting of the need, for nannies, gardeners, servants, indeed, for service, had resurrected a way of life and suppositions which a decade earlier had seemed moribund. It calmed Kate's nerves to snuff the autumn air among what she now thought of as 'her own people'.

Mrs Lure also relished Saturday morning in Gainshurst. Leisure was what Mrs Lure valued; it gave her the feeling of moneyed freedom which she knew to be her right but which life had cheated her of. Never slovenly, she did her hair with even more elaborate attention on Saturday than on weekdays, took her basket with its embroidered raffia flowers and sallied forth from her semi on the ambiguous border where Gainshurst became Cray Martyr. It would, in truth, have been more convenient to shop at Asda in Cray Martyr but that would not have been a pleasure. Better to pay a bit more and enjoy it, have someone serve you, give you a bit of attention and a chat and a bit of deference, than to have to fight one's way through the hefty womenfolk and their tribes of screaming brats in Cray Martyr.

Mrs Lure felt that success, which she equated with desert, had eluded her unfairly. Mr Lure, in whom she had put her trust, had not stayed the course. He had died before he had really got going. She had looked to him to provide and he had slipped away from her one night with a heart attack leaving her to earn her own living, which she resented having to do and was indeed ill-equipped for. She knew she had not much to offer the world and felt it was unfair of the world to make any such demands. She could have made a success of a private income. She was not without interests: she was a competent needlewoman and liked a moderate amount of housekeeping, but having to earn the bread on top was unfair. Gainshurst on a Saturday morning, therefore, was by way of being her one relaxation, where she sailed into her own, her rightful place.

Gainshurst met so many tastes. It was full of people who were either disguising who they were (because they were famous) or advertising it (because they weren't but thought they might be some day). On Saturday morning women who, the rest of the week, had not a hair out of place wore headscarves to draw attention to their disguised status. Men threw off City suits but didn't quite descend to old flannels or Levis. They weren't to that degree socially secure. They wore slacks and polished brogues. They were, like Kate Wale, newly rich: they were solid in white goods, computer hardware, architecture, sales. Their solidity was marked in their cars parked round the convenient centre of St Andrew's church to whose funds they contributed generously as though to a variety of insurance. There were few children about; most were away at school.

Yet requirements for personal service, for the human touch, allowed a number of shops to flourish which less prosperous areas had surrendered to the supermarket. There was a butcher who did it all for you. The fishmonger's was a centre of social life, run by two brothers who established their credibility by wearing straw boaters and doing a comic Cockney cross talk act for the benefit of the customers. They were felt to give good value. It was here indeed that Kate came upon the Reverend Andrew Seamley buying a half of smoked salmon and controlling a small white dog on a lead. Andrew Seamley was amazed to see Kate.

'Hello, not for ages. How's it going?' His conversational style suggested extreme intimacy and complete discretion, like a good family doctor. It had been refined to meet the inevitable social need of the cleric who is known by more people than he can quite place but who is not going to admit his ignorance. Kate admired him as someone who had to strive less hard than she herself; who, in a sense, wasn't quite such an arriviste.

Kate didn't care for dogs and therefore ignored the attempts of the West Highland to introduce himself. 'Are you coming to my group this evening?'

He would never have admitted he had no idea which group she was talking about. It was a group, wasn't it? Not much dissimulation was needed to respond, 'Ladies only, I thought.'

'Women only,' Kate corrected him.

'All girls together.' He was mistakenly skittish.

'The development and affirmation of women's spirituality need all our prayers.'

'Oh quite.' It would have been called a Ladies' Prayer Circle in former times. Now they talked of spirituality. He saw Kate didn't approve and, conditioned by the cloth to hurt no one and be agreeable to everyone, he backtracked. 'Got problems of my own this evening,' he said mysteriously.

'Your tombs,' Kate hazarded.

'Nothing the weather won't cure.'

'Start a youth club.'

'They won't come. They're unclubbable. They don't want ping-pong. They'd rather get drunk on Boddingtons. Or fornicate amongst the tombs.'

Kate laughed boisterously to show her broad-mindedness.

'How's life at the cathedral?' he enquired to re-establish norms. 'I hear the Bishop's in Jedda.'

'That was last week. This week he's in Los Angeles.'

'Ah well, never a dull moment,' he said, shaking his parcel of smoked salmon at her.

'I hope Lucy's coming this evening,' Kate crooned after him.

He might or might not have heard. Kate pressed on down the high street to the baker for the rolls, the pantry for the quiches. She loved to be greeted and was in fact known to a number of people either as Leslie's wife or in her own, canon's, right. But the man at the far end of the street just outside Oddbins was only vaguely familiar. His dark hair was too long for fashion. He wore a brown leather jacket and black denims. He was leaning back against a large rusty car parked on a double yellow. As she passed, the back door of the car swung open and another man of the same age similarly dressed stepped out. Some intimation of danger must have made itself felt. Kate stepped back into the door of Oddbins as the second man tried to grab her. 'Get in, sweetheart.'

Kate screamed easily and loudly for spiders, for spilt milk of all kinds, but now her scream seemed to her hoarse and muffled. However, it was enough.

The man behind the counter shot out. The car revved and the second man leaped into the already accelerating vehicle.

The young man from Oddbins was solicitous if not tactful. 'What was that then? Bit of a domestic?'

'I've never seen either of them before. I . . .' She stopped. Was that true? Then she remembered. It was the voice which she'd heard on the phone an hour ago.

* * *

Breakfast at the Provost's Lodging had been hurried. Susan Tye was clearly on edge. Reggie came in soon after Susan and Theodora had sat down to toast and coffee. He had difficulty in remembering who Theodora was. Conversation had not been easy. Theodora was civil about the cathedral architecture. Reggie Tye expressed amazement that she'd been to early service.

'Ah, yes, Tobias Angel. We let some of the parish clergy have an altar occasionally. They like the honour.'

Theodora nodded.

'I had hoped to have a word with him but in fact my diary doesn't allow it. No rest for the wicked.'

Theodora nodded again. In what form, she wondered, had the verger delivered Father Angel's message to the Provost?

As the cathedral clock struck the three-quarter for nine forty-five Reggie murmured about work, rose and left the kitchen. The door had scarcely closed behind him when Susan leaned over. 'He's in the bedroom getting his book. In a minute he'll be setting out for the post office. Are you ready?'

Theodora hated the melodrama. 'You're sure you want this done?'

'Yes, certain. It's even more important now, don't you see? If he does it again this Saturday, it'll show he wasn't being blackmailed by . . .' She stopped, unable to use the dead man's name.

'You don't know that he is being blackmailed.' Theodora tried for one last time to point to the path of reason.

'How else can you explain . . . ? Well, anyway, please do follow him.'

Theodora thought of all the reasons why not.

'He's going out now,' Susan wailed as the front door could be heard closing.

'All right,' Theodora said to stop the wail in Susan's voice. She thought how catching hysteria was and how little defence one had against it.

'Here, take this.' Susan thrust something soft into Theodora's hand as she propelled her down the hall.

'What is it?'

'It's a disguise,' Susan whispered.

Theodora saw it was a hat, a brimmed one in dark blue felt with a chain of tiny button daisies round the crown. It was the sort of hat which could be made to fit any shape of head and might be suitable for anything from funeral to garden party.

'Don't make many of those nowadays,' Theodora breathed as Susan let her out of the side door.

Reggie Tye was in sight. He'd crossed the lawn surrounding the east end of the cathedral and was walking towards the main exit's steps which would lead him down to the crossroads and into town. Before he reached the steps, however, he swerved to the left and made for the diocesan office block to the south side. Reggie was wearing drill trousers and a linen jacket, a panama hat and a clerical black shirt and collar. There won't be large numbers dressed like that, at any rate, Theodora thought. She lingered by the parked cars and the charabanc of a pilgrimage party. Why don't they walk, at least up the steps, Theodora thought bitterly. Hell's teeth, what on earth was she doing spending her precious free time acting out the fantasies of an old and clearly deranged school friend?

After what seemed like five hours, but perhaps was not more than five minutes, Reggie emerged and proceeded down the steps. Theodora left it as long as she dared and then hurried to the top. She was just in time to see him cross the roundabout and turn down the high street. She took the steps a lot faster than Reggie had done.

Even so, when she got to the high street, he was nowhere to be seen. Theodora had no relish for the task but, having taken it on, she was angry to fall at the first fence. She was handicapped by not knowing the terrain. Where was the post office? She scanned both sides of the street but nothing declared itself. She began to walk slowly down the right-hand side. The high street terminated in a small paved square, a pedestrianized area, with a fountain in its midst. She had almost reached this when she glanced into the interior of a chemist's shop. There it was, one of these newfangled POs located inside another shop to add to the confusion, doubtless, of both sorts of customer. And there was Reggie chatting to someone in the queue at the second guichet. Loath to let him get away again, Theodora took a chance on the way he'd turn when he came out and stationed herself further up the street on the understanding Reggie would return the way he'd come once he'd transacted his business.

This was the less fashionable end of the high street. There were few shops, more offices and little pedestrian traffic. Theodora stepped across the road to the dry cleaner's which had a large window which reflected the opposite side of the street very well. Reggie emerged from the post office and hesitated only a moment. Then he went into the haberdasher's, Misses M and C Calvert.

What on earth would Reggie want in a haberdasher's? Reggie was not the sort of man to sew on his own buttons. Theodora kept her eye on the reflection in the cleaner's window. After a minute or two Reggie came out. Theodora considered her choices. Finally, she recrossed the street and looked in the haberdasher's window. Reggie was ambling slowly back towards the cathedral. He seemed safely set for a return home. In which case perhaps she ought to check what he'd been doing.

The window had a display of knitting needles arranged in the shape of a wheel. Not too much of a clue there. Theodora clapped the felt hat on her head and pushed the haberdasher's door. A loose-standing bell tinkled above her head as she stepped over the threshold. Once inside, however, there was total silence of a long-standing variety. The light was not strong and the air a kind of pale grey. As her eyes grew accustomed to the change, she found herself eyeball to eyeball with two faces, one behind the counter and one in front. They were both, she reckoned, weighing probabilities, female, though in the dim light of the shop she couldn't be confident. There was a certain androgynous quality about them as though they might be men in drag. There was a feeling of interruption, of work suspended, of mysteries desecrated by her unholy presence.

'I'm so sorry,' Theodora murmured, sensitive as always to religious atmosphere and urgently wishing to withdraw. She glanced behind her out through the half glass door with its net curtains softening the unhallowed light. A clerical shadow which looked very like Reggie loomed on the outside. Returned for what purpose? Pray God he did not enter. Theodora was aware of a space which was higher than it was wide. Indeed its ceiling appeared to be hidden in cloud. What was she doing here, what should she be looking for, what should her questions be? It was at times like this that Theodora knew very well she was not a sleuth. She gazed at the counter for inspiration. It was of the solid polished mahogany which is no longer fitted in shops. It had a brass measuring rod sunk into it and a collecting box for Guide Dogs for the Blind at the far end.

'Can I help you, madam?' The voice too could have been male or female. It came from the figure behind the counter.

Well, at least my hat fits me for the part, Theodora thought, taking courage.

'I'm, I'm, er, just starting to learn crocheting,' she said composedly. 'I'm looking for a number two Hepplewaite cronque.' This was clearly an acceptable approach. It had the effect of galvanizing activity on the part of both the figures. With unexpected agility the one on the serving side of the counter reached for a set of steps, propped them against the wall of diminishing wooden boxes which lined the back of the shop and scuttled upwards. Thick grey-clad ankles in the sort of buckled sandals children wore in the 1950s were all that was visible. The ladder wobbled a bit with the ardour of the search.

'Cissie, dear, could you just steady the steps for me?'

The figure on Theodora's side of the counter sprang round with alacrity to aid her colleague or, perhaps, sister. After a moment's activity on both their parts the ladder-sealer descended red-faced but triumphant.

'Lovely.' Theodora summoned enthusiasm with no difficulty at all.

'Of course, we don't have the ivory ones any more. It's illegal to shoot elephants now,' the victorious one said, offering a piece of information which might not be to hand. 'But this is quite serviceable.' Theodora agreed it probably was. The cronque was lovingly wrapped in tissue paper and placed in a brown bag.

'That will be twenty-three shillings and sixpence in proper money.'

This foxed Theodora.

'Or, as we have to say nowadays, one pound seventeen and a half pence.' The old woman's face crinkled like grey tissue paper with real humour.

Theodora handed over one pound twenty with, she hoped, not too much rapidity and made for the door.

'I hope you make good progress, dear. Remember we are happy to meet all your needs. It's nice to see young people carrying on the old ways.'

'Yes, indeed. Thank you. A remarkable find,' Theodora murmured as she let herself out. It's the hat what did it, she thought, as she whipped it from her head and scanned both sides of the street. She was in luck. Reggie was on the far side with his back to her. The number 94 maroon and cream

Giltchrist to Cray Martyr via Gainshurst scooped him up before she could plan.

'There'll be another along in a minute,' said a friendly woman with a lot of shopping as she galloped up to the stop. Theodora didn't believe her and cursed herself for incompetence. She turned back up the high street and a number 94 maroon and cream Giltchrist to Cray Martyr via Gainshurst bowled towards her.

'They come in twos,' said her informant complacently.

* * *

Lionel's Saturday ritual never, if he could help it, varied. He rose at seven, cleaned his flat, collected his shirts from the laundry at the corner, ate fish cakes for breakfast by way of a treat and was at the stable by nine. It was a half-hour's bicycle ride to reach the undulating country to the north of Giltchrist and west of Cray Martyr. He thought of his ride, as he'd thought of reconnaissance trips in the army, as moving through a series of challenges and opportunities. The challenges were physical in this case, the hill from Giltchrist to the edges of Cray Martyr; the opportunities were cultural, a move from one set of values and one history to another. The very air of Cray Martyr was sharp and lawless.

Lionel remembered one occasion when, rather earlier than usual, a summer morning when no traffic stirred, he had turned the blind corner into Cray Martyr's high street and come face to face with two horses, their sharp unshod hooves rapping on the sets of the road. Their eyes were wary and confident, purposeful as they kept time with each other. As Lionel braked his bicycle to let them pass, he looked left and saw another pair, a mare with a well-grown foal at foot, all of them shades of bay with blue wall-eyes prominent from inbreeding. They were not exactly in collection but they held themselves together to give an impression of discipline as though, without human help, they could collaborate to gain their own ends. The four fell into a double column, like cavalry, their pace unvarying as they made for the open country. The beat of the hooves echoed in the dead silent street in the way it must have for centuries before the car. Lionel had felt a sense of complicity and collusion with them. Doors had opened cautiously and people gazed at them. No one tried to impede them or round them up. 'Escaped from somewhere,' Lionel had said aloud.

'Lees' yard,' said an old man standing at the door of his terrace cottage. 'They don't mend their fences, just add a prop or two. Tangle a bit more wire. A keen pony can push its way through Lees' rubbish.'

'Where are they going?' Lionel had asked. 'They seem to know.'

'They've smelt the hay they're cutting on Cray Common. They're after a mouthful.'

Lionel loved the idea of the horses smelling, plotting, pushing their unreliable fences and trotting out in orderly fashion to fill their basic needs. What more do human beings achieve, after all? What else is freedom?

Lionel remembered the scene every time he passed the end of the common. He had indeed formed the habit of making the short detour to take in the Lees' fields. Today he pedalled past slowly, half looking for Mick Lee's van. There it stood in the corner of the field abutting the last council house on the track which led to the main road. Outside there was a boy of about ten washing or cleaning something. Two ponies were grazing in the far corner. The other half of the field was a scrapyard, full of decrepit car chassis. Lionel wondered whether he ought to stop and visit Mrs Lee. But no, he'd do that at the proper time. Monday would be soon enough.

Instead he turned down the rutted track to his own stable. He cut his speed to deal with the potholes. He always thought that the way in which a country building filled the potholes in its approach roads was an indication of the quality of the institution. This one had done its best with crushed plant pots from the nursery next door plus woodshavings from the saw mill behind them. He smelt the familiar delicious smell of the well-kept muck heaps.

There was such a difference between yards, he thought. He remembered the three ponies in a lean-to shed and an over-grazed paddock with a bath in the corner where he'd learned to ride as a boy, and then the grand purpose-built immaculate quarters of the army stables in Germany, with sanded manèges. His current stable lay somewhere between the two extremes. He named it to himself as 'south circular pretentious'. It catered for the sort of people in Gainshurst who wanted to ride using the slatternly labour of Cray Martyr. That is to say the stable boys were girls without money and the clients were girls with money who spent a lot on riding gear and fancy tack; who had, in fact, more money than horse sense. The clientele specialized in spindly Arab chestnut mares. All more trouble than they were worth, in Lionel's opinion. Gainshurst Equestrian Centre, said the signpost. Lionel's theory was that the owner couldn't spell the word 'stable'.

But for all the outward shortcomings of the place, when he'd first come to Giltchrist, to his job at the diocesan office, he'd been very content to find this particular establishment. It had been apparent that he couldn't afford to keep a horse of his own at full livery at the current rates. So he'd looked round for a good stable to provide him with someone to share with. Weekends were spent cycling round the countryside assessing the local yards. Finally he'd hit on Gainshurst Equestrian Centre. He'd looked at the beds; they were deep whether with straw or chippings. He'd looked at the hay, which was sweet and plentiful. He'd looked at the grass and seen smooth five-inch-long turf without a stem of ragwort in sight. Managing grassland for grazing for thirty horses is a task for the expert. Lionel's heart leapt up when he saw it. This was no amateur establishment whatever its fancy name. Someone knew what they were doing. It made a change from the office.

He talked, in the end and with some difficulty, to the proprietor, a taciturn woman, four foot by four foot, who was not looking for clients. However, after a bit of preliminary toing and froing she agreed to give him a month's trial. He found himself elated as though accepted into a club he wanted to join. And so it proved. It was a club, one as remote in values and ethos from the diocesan office as it was possible to find. Horses, if you will let them, Lionel thought, have the effect of earthing people. 'Humilis', earthy, Lionel remembered his prep school Latin. The Church on the other hand seems to puff people up, making demands on them beyond, for the most part, their moral capacity and corrupting them in their talentlessness with more power than they know how to handle.

He had set about finding himself a horse with the remains of his army gratuity. At first he'd thought Vincent might come in with him. But Vincent hadn't been much of a rider. He could just about stick on if he needed to. Later of course Vincent had been unavailable. In the end he'd found a mare and a friend all in one go.

The mare was a flighty, uneducated, sixteen-hand, dark bay seven-year-old, pretty and spoilt, a woman's horse, except for her height. But she had good bone and a short back and a pretty bottom. 'What's she done?' Lionel had asked the ritual question expecting the ritual answer: 'A bit of everything,' which meant nothing or cubbing. But the owner, a vacant-eyed girl who had moved on from horses to boys, said honestly, 'Well, what she's mostly done is go in straight lines very fast.' 'Does she jump?' Lionel had pursued. 'Not if she can help it,' the honest girl had replied. Lionel had paid her in cash, five hundred less than she had asked but the sight of actual money had excited her.

If the mare was flighty, the friend, George Lawley, was the opposite. He was a man of total integrity, utterly without pretension, quiet, with his own large grey gelding. Both horse and man were methodical, thorough, reliable. George never claimed knowledge he didn't have and everything he did he did competently and without fuss. He had a small carpenter's business which did a lot of restoration work for Gainshurst's antiques trade. He made enough money to satisfy his family's needs and refused to expand and make more. 'My lads can expand, if they want, when their time comes,' was his line. Since his lads were seven and nine at St Sylvester and St Andrew's CE-Aided Primary School on the edge of Cray Martyr, this was not imminent.

Lionel had met George when George had been delivering a load of chippings for the stable proprietor. It emerged that he rode out three times a week and wanted some tuition over the cross-country course because he was self-taught and he lacked, he said, style. Would Lionel give him a lesson or two for a consideration? Lionel thought this was a good way of earning a bit for the livery instead of having to share his mare with anyone. He took his duties seriously and scrupulously put George and his powerful grey over fences every Wednesday night. Saturday and Sunday mornings they hacked out together through the woods to the north of the stable which surrounded and disguised Gainshurst. Then they went to the Plume of Feathers to finish off. It was an undemanding friendship based on mutual respect, which suited them both.

This Saturday, Lionel was late. The two horses, George's grey and Lionel's bay, were already out of their boxes and short-racked in the standings at the end of the yard. A number of heads hopefully seeking treats, or, failing that, owners, appeared over half-doors of boxes as Lionel braked on the black brick surface. George had started grooming his grey. The yard was empty of people.

'Made a detour to see the Lees' ponies,' Lionel explained, pushing carrots into the mare and taking his grooming kit considerately placed by George out from between her legs.

'Nasty business, your young Lee getting smashed. Just when he was getting on his feet.'

They groomed their horses side by side, both with quick rhythmic strong strokes of brush and curry, a ballet of movement. It was part of the joint shared pleasure of soldier and carpenter.

'Which feet would those be?'

'That bit of land. Your neck of the woods. Behind the church, St Sylvester's.'

'What about it?'

'Lees have been there on and off for a long time.'

'So I imagine.'

'Leslie Wale tried to get the Lees off that land so he could sell it for the bypass.'

'When?'

'When they were all just starting out.'

'Who's all?'

'Leslie Wale of Wale Holdings. Only he didn't hold so much then. Ten years ago, perhaps.'

'Before my time,' Lionel said comfortably, doing a brisk job on the mare's tangled mane.

'Rumour was, Lees claimed they owned that land and Father Angel helped them fight Wale off.'

'What was Tobias Angel doing helping the Lees?'

'Everyone thought the land belonged to the church, but Angel said no, the Lees had title.'

'Well, the bypass came to nothing.' Lionel transferred his attention to the tail which had pieces of straw plaited in it.

'Still, not a good start in commercial life in Cray Martyr to make an enemy of the Lees.' George was judicious as he carefully sponged the grey's nostrils. 'Why don't you use a dandy first?'

'Because she's got a thoroughbred's coat and it would hurt her. I'd no idea Kate Wale's husband dealt in that sort of thing.' Lionel squatted down to pick out hooves and hurried to catch up with George. He looked up between his mare's legs. 'Are you sure that's right?'

George preferred narration to argument. 'A very bright lad, our Leslie. Could I borrow your curry a tick? Thanks. Mother was a hairdresser in a back street of Cray Martyr. But she was always a high stepper and she pushed the lad after dad died. Or did he leave? I forget.'

'I suppose the Lees and the Wales must be of an age. Do you want hoof oil?'

'I prefer tar on a grey. Sets them off nicely against the coat, in my opinion.'

'Dries the wall out, in the long run, in my opinion.' Lionel loved these interchanges with George.

'Wale's come a long way. Left the Lees far behind. Great big house in Church Crescent, BMW, holidays in the Greek isles. The works. Can that be done honestly?'

'I never thought. I suppose I've only met Leslie once and I think of Kate as a sort of spectator sport, not really a serious person, a lightweight, like so many of them, pretending most of the time, not capable of doing serious harm any more than they could do serious good.'

'Well, her bloke's serious. I wouldn't cross Leslie Wale in a deal.'

'And the Lees did?'

'Not so much cross as disoblige, stood up for their rights. It'll be interesting to see how things pan out, now Mick Lee's dead.'

They had come to the point when it was a matter of standing back and admiring their handiwork. Simultaneously they reached for saddles and bridles propped on the wooden standings. They could have been doing it to music, they were both so methodical; not hurried, not slow, as men who know what they are doing and that there are ways of doing things properly.

'Were you ever in the forces?' Lionel asked. He realized he didn't know much of George's past.

'No, though I had a spell in the scouts,' George acknowledged. 'But mostly I'm nothing more than a carpenter.'

'Couldn't be better,' Lionel acknowledged.

The bay gleamed as only a bay can. The grey looked clean and laundered. George allowed himself the frippery of a bit of plaiting on the tail. The two men mounted together. Together bridles clinked, clean leather squeaked and the iron-shod hooves rattled the brick as they left the yard.

Why didn't I know all this about Lee, Lionel asked himself. But then Archdeacon Marcus More was the diocesan officer responsible for everything to do with land ownership and he was close. Would he and Leslie Wale agree a land deal to make money by dispossessing a family like the Lees? And if so might that have resulted in Lee's death?

* * *

'So Reggie did draw out as usual.'

'Well, I can't be absolutely sure. He went to the post office, then went on to Gainshurst.'

'Right.'

'I did my best.' Theodora thought, why should I have to justify an expertise I never claimed and did not want to exercise in the first place?

'You caught the Gainshurst bus though.' Susan was going to go through the whole thing.

'Yes. When I got there, I spotted Reggie in the high street chatting to a rather handsome man in a clerical collar with a West Highland on a lead.'

'Andrew Seamley from St Andrew's has a West Highland. Then what?'

'They turned and went back towards the church at the other end of the high street. St Andrew's. On the way they stopped to speak to a woman with a large raffia-embroidered shopping bag.'

'What did she look like?'

'Short, middle-aged, purple dress and crocheted white wool shawl. Body language suggested they all knew each other quite well.'

Susan was impressed by this. If she'd hired Theodora this was the sort of knowledge she would have been paying for. 'I wonder if it might have been Mrs . . .'

'A very elaborate hairdo, coils and combs and things.'

'Mrs Lure,' said Susan, this time without hesitation. 'Veronica Lure. She's secretary to Reggie and Marcus More. Then what?'

'I waited about outside the church until about eleven thirty, then Reggie came out and made for the bus stop. He caught the first ninety-four back and I caught the second.'

Susan Tye put the apple parings into newspaper and started to clear the kitchen table for lunch. 'So do we know if Reggie has passed the money on or has he still got it?'

'I've no idea.'

'Did he look as if he was passing brown envelopes to Andrew Seamley or Mrs Lure?'

'I really don't know.' Theodora was impatient with this grilling. 'Why don't you just ask Reggie?'

'How could I do that without admitting I'd looked in his collar box and read his PO book?'

Theodora saw the point. 'How much has Reggie got?'

'He's not a rich man. We've actually always had to live off his stipend. And of course we have to keep up a certain standard of entertaining in Reggie's present position.'

Theodora contemplated the chaotic kitchen and recalled the appalling supper and wondered what standard that would be.

'I mean we could do with that thousand.'

Theodora thought of the free house, free car and seventeen thousand a year pocket money which a provost's stipend entitled him to. It dissipated any pity she might have had for Reggie. 'What about approaching it from the other end? What could Reggie ever have done which could initiate blackmail? And then who would know of it?'

'I wondered,' Susan was pensive, 'whether it would be possible for you to question his colleagues in the cathedral just to see if you get a feel about any of them? Archdeacon More and Kate Wale, for example.'

'I can hardly go up to a complete stranger like Marcus More and say, "Oh, by the way, do you know any reason why the Provost should be being blackmailed? And are you by any chance the one who's doing it?"'

'Well, perhaps not quite like that, but you are very skilled. I expect if you got talking . . .'

'I can see absolutely no way,' said Theodora forcefully.

'But you could make a start. How do you eat an elephant?' Susan was quoting from her latest counselling course.

'Little by little,' Theodora answered dourly.

'Exactly. I thought we could make a start. We could go to Kate Wale's spirituality group this evening. You could have a word with her there.'

'But I've never met the woman.'

'Oh, you'll like her. She's got lots of go. Everyone gets on with Kate.'

'No, Susan, I'm not going.' Theodora was quite firm.

CHAPTER SIX: SEARCHING

'This is Theodora Braithwaite. Canon Kate Wale,' said Susan Tye.

Theodora and Kate looked at each other with simultaneous dislike. Both tried to hide this from themselves and from each other, for the greater good.

Kate said, 'Hi. Wonderful to see you.'

Theodora said, 'How do you do?'

Theodora took in Canon Wale's dress, accent and scent. Canon Wale took in Theodora's lack of these things. Theodora wore an ancient brown dress which she'd tracked down in Mencap in Betterhouse. She never wore scent and her accent had been formed in another milieu than Kate's. Kate was marvellously attired in a scarlet woollen dress with long flowing sleeves like a bachelor's gown. Gold bangles, heavy and clanking, clashed on both arms. Theodora had about ten inches' advantage on Canon Wale. And that's all she's got, thought Kate who immediately became an effusive hostess.

They were standing in the hall of Kate's Gainshurst house. It contrasted sharply with the Provost's Lodging. The parquet shone. The Oriental mats were deep. There was a smell of percolating coffee from the drawing room. The murmur of women's voices came from within, subdued but animated, let off the leash perhaps, Theodora thought.

'You're more than welcome,' Kate enthused. 'Do come through.'

More welcome than what and through what, Theodora asked herself, noting idioms which she despised and taking refuge, as always, in linguistic analysis to drown the embarrassment of this ghastly woman. Through fire and water, through thick and thin?

In the drawing room, which was forty foot long and furnished in the sort of pale colours, peach, beige, which are only possible if you have no children, ample domestic help and lots of money, were gathered about a dozen women of various sizes. Some sat in the deep armchairs and sofas, some on cushions on the floor, which was perhaps making some sort of statement since there was ample seating for all.

'Everybody,' cried Kate, calling them to order, 'Susan you all know, of course, and this is Theo. May I call you Theo? Well, we'll go round names and contexts before we start as per usual. Has everyone got everything they want? Coffee? Supper in an hour.'

It was clear these pronouncements were ritual. Kate called them, others obeyed them. Was this going to be the pattern, Theodora wondered. Was this what the session was set up for? Theodora had never been to a women's spirituality group before. Her many duties in her urban parish, her one hobby (scholarly research into the life of the Tractarian Thomas Henry Newcome, founder of the Order of St Sylvester), left her little time for extras. Anyway, she wasn't sure there could be a separate spirituality for men and women. The disciplines of the spiritual life, the life lived from and towards the Christian triune God, were the same for all: they comprised prayer, worship, sacrament, meditation on scripture, and support of the faithful community. These could not be different for men and women. What alternative path were these people, these women, about?

Kate seated herself on a large cushion on the floor. Susan Tye perched on the edge of an armchair. Theodora looked round for an upright and folded herself into the only wooden chair.

'Shall we pray?' Kate invited. Because of Kate's vowel sounds Theodora thought she said 'pry' and then banished the thought that this might be an omen. She took herself in hand. I've got to be more open, more tolerant of styles other than my own, she resolved.

They did pray or rather Kate did at length and apparently spontaneously. The sentences lurched. God was addressed as 'You' and told a lot of things He presumably already knew, like 'You have brought us together here at this moment in time', and other things which were only dubiously true like 'we are all just very grateful for this time just to be here together with each other'.

When Kate had finished, there was a moment's silence and then a voice which Theodora tracked down to a large woman deep in a sofa said, 'Shall we share?'

There was a rustle of approval, corsets loosened.

'Yes,' said Kate, obviously determined not to let things out of her own hands. 'Let's welcome our newcomers. Shall we tell them who we are and perhaps a tiny bit about ourselves?' Theodora suppressed a shudder at the coyness.

The women were clearly agog to do this. Theodora, who by this time had abandoned resolves to be tolerant and was concentrating on resisting the temptation to put her hands over her ears and rock to and fro in her chair to dissipate the embarrassment, decided she had no intention of ever seeing any of these women again and determined to survive by observing the social tensions.

'I'm Melanie,' said the first sharer, as though this in itself must be a point in her favour. Erroneously, thought Theodora. 'I'm just a typist,' she said with pride.

They went round the circle. It was impossible to remember or discriminate. Most defined themselves by their jobs. Then, 'A widow,' said one. Is that a job, Theodora wanted to ask but didn't. A wife and mother, a pharmacist, a receptionist followed. Susan Tye said, 'I'm a clergy wife. I support my husband.' They were all in their forties or fifties. Theodora thought how much more interesting it might be if they were to define themselves by their main virtues and vices. For a moment she thought of saying Theodora Braithwaite, vice arrogance, virtue humility. But discretion prevailed and she stuck to 'curate'.

'Well, I think that shows we're all in the service industries,' said Kate when they'd finished. It was clearly a dearly loved joke. 'I think we all know but our new members might like to be filled in on it, we're all here . . .' Kate's voice grew in emotion and authority as she spoke. 'We're all here,' she repeated, 'to affirm our own being.'

Well, at least she's honest, Theodora thought. No nonsense about God to cloud the issue.

'To affirm our own being,' Kate continued, 'in a hostile environment. There's a great deal in the world which wants to diminish us, to make us seem little. But we aren't. We're big. We're very, very big. Let's just pause there and imagine all the ways in which we're big.'

Kate put a lot of emphasis on this word and stretched her arms in their big red sleeves wide and yet wider so that the woman next to her held tightly on to her coffee cup. There was a couple of minutes' silence during which Theodora went through all the ways in which she disagreed with this statement theologically as a description of any human being in the light of eternity. Theodora, a connoisseur of silence, preferred to consider the quality of that silence. It was strained, a shade embarrassed, not yet quite at ease with itself. She could hear one member of the group sniffing compulsively, which would defeat most silences, she reckoned.

'Now we're going to try to imagine how Love will cope with our feelings of littleness.'

'Love' was clearly spelt with a capital in Kate's voice. 'How do we cope with feeling little? Let's imagine a little, tiny thing which we value very, very much and think what,' she paused, 'Love would say to it.'

Theodora thought this was an incomprehensible demand so she listened to the silence again. She was, therefore, the first to be aware of the sound of a car crunching on the generous gravel and the bang of the front door. Theodora had got as far as wondering whether the sound was unnaturally loud because of the silence or because of the force applied to it when the drawing room door burst open. A man stood in it for a moment. He had no tie. His lilac shirt was torn from top button to trouser top and the white flesh beneath looked blue as though from bruising. The sleeve of his dark blue business suit jacket hung off at the shoulder. His floppy brown hair was streaked with liquid — sweat or water — and plastered either side of his face. From a cut lip blood ran disregarded down his chin. Kate swung round and, for the second time that day, screamed.

'Leslie.'

The man slid down the door jamb on to the brightly polished parquet.

* * *

It was too late, Susan Tye said to Theodora on the drive home, to do anything that night. 'But we must do our best to help Kate tomorrow. Something's up. I didn't believe that story about Leslie having slipped on one of the building sites, did you?'

'It seemed unlikely, since she didn't have time to ask him before she told us,' Theodora agreed.

'It's time you took on a proper investigation.'

Theodora did not believe she was hearing aright. 'Investigation of what?'

'Reggie's being blackmailed—'

'We don't know that for certain.'

Susan went on as though Theodora hadn't spoken. 'Reggie's being blackmailed, Mick Lee's been murdered. And now Leslie's been done over. It all hangs together.'

'That's absolute nonsense. There need be no connection between any of these incidents.'

'So, I think first thing tomorrow you need to get your act together,' Susan was severe, as though Theodora had up to now been slacking, 'and do some private eying. I'll ring Kate in the morning and you can go and see her and start from there.'

There was no point, Theodora reflected, in arguing with the mad. What she wanted now was proper prayer and bed. She regretted they'd not got round to supper at Kate's.

'How about fishing and chipping?' she asked without hope.

But Susan unexpectedly relented. They swerved round via Giltchrist high street and joined the post-pub queue at the chippie in the square.

Lionel, four places in front of them, waved cheerily. He'd had exactly the sort of day he liked.

'Can I get you something?' he called back to them.

They stood round the fountain in the middle of the square and ate out of the paper like teenagers.

'I've just been to see *The Mikado*,' Lionel confided.

'"If you want to know who we are",' Theodora hummed.

'Yes. They were wonderful. Not too gifted vocally but such attack. I do love provincial pleasures.'

'We've just been to Kate Wale's women's spirituality group,' said Theodora to see how he would cope.

'A spectator sport in herself,' Lionel agreed.

They told him about the drama of Leslie's return.

'I've told Theodora to get her finger out,' Susan said.

Theodora concluded the unusual amount of food consumed by her hostess had gone to her head like strong drink.

'What finger? Why Theodora?' Lionel not unnaturally enquired.

'Theodora's a gumshoe, a sleuth, a private eye,' Susan said with pride.

Theodora's smooth manners deserted her. 'I'm nothing of the kind. Don't be such a crackpot.'

'Yes you are, yes you are,' Susan Tye chanted. They had both slipped back to the level of the fifth form.

Lionel was quite cheered by this, even though he was unsure whether they were joking or not. 'What do you want investigated?' he asked Susan.

Susan was caught off guard. She said, 'Reggie's blackmail, Mick Lee's death and Leslie's accident,' before she could think. There was a moment's silence while Lionel considered whether he should pretend that he hadn't heard this. Curiosity got the better of him.

'I didn't know Reggie was in trouble.'

Theodora thought the least she could do was rescue her hostess. 'He may not be being blackmailed.'

'He is, he is, poor Reggie,' his wife wailed.

Theodora reviewed the evidence for Lionel. She had expected him to laugh the tissue of improbabilities away. Instead, however, he said to Susan, 'Did you know that Leslie Wale had a previous run-in with the Lee family over the question of the new bypass and their land?'

'When?'

'Oh, some time ago, about ten years or so, when Wale was just starting out.'

'There you are,' Susan said to Theodora, 'I told you so.'

'You told me nothing of the kind.'

'No, I know I didn't tell you about that. How could I have known? I mean I told you Lee's death was connected with Leslie's "accident".'

'We have absolutely no shred of evidence that it was anything of the kind,' Theodora insisted. 'And even less evidence that Reggie is being blackmailed by anyone or that it has anything to do with Lee's death *or* Leslie's accident.'

Susan turned the full searchlight of her emotions upon Lionel and said, 'Lionel, my best friend deserts me in my hour of need. But you won't, will you? We've known each other a long time. Please help me?'

Lionel, Theodora was glad to see, was embarrassed. Never trust a man incapable of embarrassment.

He said suddenly, 'I'm going to see my brother tomorrow. One of his colleagues in jail is a man called Elvestone, the man who owned the scaffolding company before Wale Holdings took it over. It's just possible we could learn something from that source.' He turned to Theodora. 'Would you care to come with me? Sometimes a clerical collar can oil wheels.'

Theodora thought Susan might feel excluded by the invitation, which had been offered in a way which definitely excluded her. But Susan said, 'Please go, Theo. If you can find out anything which can help Reggie I'd be so grateful.'

* * *

The prison at Fordingham, forty miles west of Giltchrist, was set in proper country amidst gentle hills which would eventually join up with the Cotswolds. The sky was dark grey and full of rain which thickened in the course of the afternoon. As they completed the miles, chugging along in Lionel's veteran vehicle, orchestrated by the punctilious movements of his driving, Theodora was aware of how increasingly tense Lionel was. The tic which she had noticed during her first car journey with him had returned. To try to relax him she started to ask questions.

'How did your brother come to be in Cray Martyr the night of the accident?'

'He had a small architect's practice in Gainshurst. On the night the accident happened he was coming from Gainshurst to Giltchrist.'

'To see you?'

Lionel was silent. 'Do you know,' he said at length, 'I never asked. I just assumed that was so.'

Theodora hadn't thought her question in the least important. Now she thought it worth pursuing. 'How did the accident happen exactly?'

'As he tells it,' Lionel said, 'Vincent was coming round the corner from the main Gainshurst to Giltchrist road by the pub, the Plume of Feathers. We passed it on Friday evening when I picked you up. There's no way of avoiding it unless you go a very long way round.'

'Right.' Theodora marvelled that Lionel could make the journey with equanimity.

'The pub was loosing and there was a crowd spilling out into the road. There was a fight going on and there were about a dozen blokes blocking the way. Vincent started to edge through and one of them banged on the roof of the car and handled the door. Vincent says his foot slipped on the accelerator and the next thing he knew he had a man on his bonnet. The police arrived about the same time and when they took the man up he was dead. Blow below the heart, supposedly from the car radiator, had killed him.'

Theodora nodded. Lionel had increased the speed of the car in time with his emotions.

She had to ask, 'Did you know Mick Lee was working as a scaffolder on the cathedral?'

Lionel did not take his eye from the road. 'No,' he said, 'no, why should I? At the trial the man who gave evidence to identify the body was Deke Lee, the eldest brother. Though, in fact, it was the police evidence which did for Vincent. They'd breathalysed him and they seemed to think it was more important that Vince was a bit over the limit than to discover any other fact at all. No,' Lionel went on, 'it's odd to think I watched Mick Lee day after day and said hello to him and never knew my brother had killed his brother. It makes a bond of a sort, doesn't it?'

Theodora carefully analysed the tone. It was not that she distrusted Lionel, it was simply that she did not know him well enough to know what he was feeling.

Lionel saved her the trouble of a reply by slowing down and fumbling in his pocket. The sign said 'Visitors' Car Park'. Lionel handed a pass to a shrivelled walnut of a man dressed in tweeds who seemed to know Lionel.

'As though we were doing a National Trust picnic,' said Lionel bitterly. 'They make us park half a mile away and walk. If you're related to a criminal you must be a criminal and due for a bit of punishment as well.'

Theodora could see this was not going to be an easy visit. What a way to spend a Sunday afternoon, she thought, and then, well, it's all experience and perhaps we might learn something about Mick Lee's death or Reggie's blackmail or Leslie Wale.

Outside, the buildings more resembled a country club or one of the more rigorous health farms than a prison. Theodora had visited prisons in the course of her parish duties as a curate in south London. This didn't look at all like Pentonville. There was an absence of razor wire or high walls. The centre was a grey brick Victorian building not unlike Theodora's preparatory school. At a distance were four long greenhouses and a cluster of demountables.

'Do you come often?' she asked Lionel.

'As often as I'm allowed.'

'Which is?'

'Since he's become a trustie, every eight weeks.'

'What do you do to become a trustie?'

'The same as you do in any total institution, boarding school, army, hospital: keep your head down and your nose clean.'

They got out of the car and Lionel walked purposefully across the patch of weedy gravel towards the exit. There were a number of other cars, a couple of vans and a battered Range Rover. Two large black Labradors looked keen and indignant, as only Labradors can, as the door closed on them. Lionel nodded curtly to the pair, a man and a woman, climbing down from the Range Rover. The man wore tweeds, the woman a Barbour, wellies and a Hermès headscarf. The feel was midway between the more disreputable point to point and a car boot sale.

'Willie comes out in a month, on parole,' said the woman to Lionel in an accent which did not suggest the criminal classes.

'Good for him.' Lionel's tone was hearty but forced.

'When does your brother . . . ?' she enquired tactfully.

'Two and a half years,' Lionel answered bleakly.

'I'm so sorry. I'm sure the comforts of the Church are a great support.' She had glanced at Theodora's collar, which, as Lionel had suggested, she had donned for the occasion.

At the front of the house they waited. It was a quarter to two. At half past two the door opened and a jolly, fatherly looking man in a sort of traffic warden's uniform with a very white short-sleeved nylon shirt said, 'All passes must be shown. Have your passes ready.'

'I rang and put you on the list as the Reverend Braithwaite. He'll expect a man. So it'll be nice for him to have a surprise.' Clearly this was the tone Lionel assumed to get himself through this ordeal, Theodora thought.

The queue of about a dozen people was orderly, embarrassed, in part truculent. One woman lacked a pass. There was an altercation. It held up the rest. The woman was parted from the queue and waited patiently while the others filed in front of her.

The hall was so familiar Theodora wondered if she hadn't been here before. There was the smell of cabbage and Dettol. Only the honours boards were lacking. A portrait of the Queen in the uniform of a highland regiment hung in their place. They waited again. Twenty minutes is a long wait with nowhere to sit down. Then a door at the far end was opened with a flourish. Names were called and one by one the visitors were allowed into what must have been the dining room of the original house. It was stripped bare of any finery now. There were five deal tables each with three chairs, one on one side and two on the other. Round the walls, in place of the original suits of armour, stood men in the same sort of uniform as the greeter. Lionel, who naturally knew the form, made for the table nearest the door and sat down. No one spoke. Then the door at the other end of the room was opened and names were called, this time of prisoners. One by one they came in, locked their gaze on to the faces of those they were looking for and came up to the tables.

A tall ruddy-faced man in dark blue overalls paused for a moment by the entrance and then strode over to Lionel's table and sat down.

'My dear fellow, how enormously nice to see you.' Vincent grinned from ear to ear. His floppy pepper and salt hair was short and not well cut. But his air was one of health and outdoor life. He was perhaps five or six years younger than his brother.

'Miss Braithwaite, I'm so glad to meet you. It's very good of you to traipse out here and endure my poor brother's driving. I'm afraid we're not allowed to shake hands in case you should pass me a file and a dollop of crack but I'm sure we can take it as read.'

Whereas Lionel's manner was self-contained and his speech allusive, Vincent's was open and unguarded.

'How goes it, brother?' Lionel asked. He looked more relaxed now that he had set eyes on Vincent.

'I've been promoted,' said Vincent proudly. 'I'm on cucumbers now.'

'Is that a good thing?'

'Oh, rather, much easier than pot plants. I really so hate pelargoniums. I was always breaking them. Cucumbers are quite sturdy little fellows with a good feel to them. Also the company's more congenial.'

'Who've you got?'

'Didn't I tell you? Elvestone.' Vincent nodded towards the table behind him. Theodora saw a fat balding man seated opposite the pair from the Range Rover. 'He's really very good company. Knows a tremendous number of people, some of them quite respectable. Full of libellous gossip. It helps to pass the time. He doesn't know a lot about cucumbers though. And how are things back at the ranch?'

'Ah,' said Lionel, 'well now, we've had a bit of drama at the office.' He paused, then got it out. 'Mick Lee came off a scaffold board up the cathedral spire on Friday afternoon. He'd been working on the restoration. The police say the board was faulty. The scaffolders were part of Leslie Wale Holdings but before that—'

'They were part of Elvestone's firm,' Vincent finished. 'How do you mean the board was faulty?'

One of the traffic wardens moved down the rows and Lionel waited until he had passed. 'The police say someone had partly cut it through.' Lionel looked at his brother. 'Vince, the night it happened, the night you . . .'

'Yes. OK. The night of the accident.' Vincent was quite composed. 'Go on.'

'Were you coming to see me?'

Vincent seemed to catch his brother's meaning. 'No,' he said slowly. 'To be honest, my dear fellow, I wasn't.'

'Then where . . . ?'

Vincent glanced round and said rapidly, 'Two things but both dangerous. I never said because I didn't want you to get drawn in. I still don't but perhaps in the light of the death of this other Lee brother you need to know.'

Vincent spoke with concentration for some time. Theodora leaned forward to catch his lowered tones. 'And the man who could probably help you most,' he concluded, 'would be our chaplain, the Rev. Tobias.'

'Father Angel?' Theodora enquired.

'The very same. You've met him?'

'Briefly.'

'He could help. The only difficulty with him is you never know whose side he's on because of the confessional.'

The officer walked back again and Vincent leaned back in his chair and smiled at Theodora as though he'd known her many years. Then he resumed. Ten minutes later the bell rang. There was a scraping of chairs and a rise in the volume of noise. Then the prisoners went out through their door and the visitors straggled out through theirs, like the last act of a play.

* * *

Lionel and Theodora drove back in silence. The grey clouds grew heavier and eventually wept their burden to the ground.

As they reached the low hills on the edge of Giltchrist, Lionel said, 'I'd very much like it if you would come in and let me talk about what Vincent said.'

'It casts another light on everything,' Theodora agreed.

'I can offer you supper in my digs. Thai or Italian?'

Theodora was impressed. She'd known several men cooks. They had all been good.

'It's a take-away service,' Lionel said, so that there should be no misunderstanding.

Theodora thought of what probably awaited her with Susan in the Provost's Lodging. She had no hesitation. 'Lovely. Thank you.' Conscience and manners smote her. 'Had I perhaps better let Susan know?'

'Ring from Honeysuckle Terrace.'

'Right.'

Lionel's rooms were bachelor sparse and military neat, and yet the feeling was one of needs catered for. There was nothing which did not serve a purpose. There were two huge club armchairs each with a small table beside it. A round table in front of the window had *The Times*, the *Church Times* and *The Field* laid out. There were two table lamps on the lower shelves of the book cases either side of the chimney piece. There were no pictures of any kind but a framed black and white photograph of a large hunter, his insolent, vacant stare looking out from a silver frame on the mantelshelf. While Lionel went off to converse with the Thai cooks on the telephone in the hall, Theodora scanned his books. The Army List, Butterworth's *Ecclesiastical Law*, Podaisky on classical equitation, Somerville and Ross, Saki, Kipling, Surtees, Waugh's *Sword of Honour* and Ford Madox Ford's Good Soldier trilogy and then on the top shelf, good heavens, a complete set of Disraeli's novels, *Lothair*, *Sybil*. Not the list of a dunce.

'Twenty minutes,' Lionel announced, returning with two good-sized glasses of pale sherry frosting in his hand. He glanced at Theodora leaning against his mantelpiece. 'Can you sum a character from its effects?' He nodded to the books.

'I wouldn't dream of trying,' Theodora defended herself.

'It's a temptation. I once got a look at my clerical boss's villa, Marcus More, on the outskirts of Giltchrist but the fashionable end, i.e. the end opposite to me. He had a complete list of Oxford Classical Texts.'

'Very impressive,' Theodora said, impressed.

'Spit new, unopened, some of them. I had a good mosey around. The only other thing he had was shelf on shelf of biographies of the great and the not so good, politicians, soldiers and the more macho archbishops. Revelatory.'

'What does Reggie have?' Theodora asked, realizing she'd not seen inside the Provost's study.

'The beginner's guide to Bible study and a recipe book or two on how to write sermons.' Lionel was dismissive.

'I knew he wasn't a scholar.'

'Not many of those in the Church,' agreed Lionel. 'Not that you need to be to conduct business properly.'

Lionel changed gear and Theodora realized the business of the evening had begun.

'What Vincent said,' Lionel began carefully, 'does not reflect well on him.'

'It's to his credit that he said it at all.' Theodora saw no point in adding misery to misery.

'It struck me, as he was talking,' Lionel said, 'that the reason he made so little fuss, so little attempt to defend himself at his trial was because he felt guilt.'

'But not guilt for the death of Jon Lee.'

'Right.' Lionel put his sherry down on his table. 'I wonder if you would allow me to recapitulate Vincent's story and then, as an impartial outsider, you could give me your views.'

'I would find that very helpful,' Theodora reassured him. She liked his formality. One knew where one was with such a style.

'On the night of Vincent's accident he was not coming from Gainshurst to Giltchrist to see me. He was coming from London. In fact he was coming from an appointment with Wale Holdings. And his intention was to meet the youngest Lee brother, Jon.'

'Right,' said Theodora.

'Wale Holdings wanted to negotiate a price for the land running from Cray Common to the back of the Plume of Feathers. Vince thinks the Lees didn't know but Wale did, that Mackenzie's All Foods wanted their first southern hypermarket there.'

'Wonderful site as far as transport goes between two main north-south trunk roads.'

'Can get their disgusting porridge down here, no problem. But . . .'

'But no outlet from site to feeder roads except via Lee land.'

'Lee-claimed land.'

'Had the brothers Lee known who wanted the land and for what purpose . . .'

'The price would have gone up. Moreover,' Lionel remembered George's tale, 'there had been a previous run-in between Wale and the Lees so it's not surprising he'd use Vincent rather than approaching the Lees himself.'

'Vincent running down one of the brothers was not a good beginning in that enterprise.'

Lionel shook his head.

'Do I gather that Vincent thinks that the Lees' title to the land isn't a sound one?' Theodora asked.

'It skirts the church.'

'Father Angel's St Sylvester's?'

'And if it were Church land not Lee land, the Church might make a packet out of it.'

'And the Lees would make nothing. Do you know Deke?'

'He has the reputation of a hard man. Do you think it's an accident that two brothers out of three who claim title to a valuable bit of land which stands in the way of a development worth millions are both dead?'

'On the other hand, Wale would benefit if he could get the land off the Lees for MAF.'

'You heard what Vince said: "There's no way I was going fast enough to kill anyone with my radiator. I was practically stationary when I heard the thud of a body landing on my bonnet. Even if you'd hurled yourself against it the most you'd have got would be bruised."'

'The difficulty with that is,' Theodora did not want to hurt Lionel but it had to be said, 'no witness came forward at the time to testify to that. It's very easy to be mistaken in a mêlée.'

'I know, I know.' Lionel suddenly sounded tired. 'But say Vince was right, not mistaken or confused, say someone did kill Jon and tossed him on to Vince's bonnet.'

'Who would do that?'

'Depends who would benefit from Lee's death.'

'The developers.'

'Wale Holdings.'

'The Church.'

'One of the other Lee brothers.'

'Then there's Vincent's other point,' Theodora said. 'He said that the Lees couldn't produce documentary evidence that they owned the land.'

'Let's take these in order,' said Lionel. There was the sound of a door knocker. 'Hang on.'

Lionel ran downstairs very fast. Hope I still have that speed at sixty-five, Theodora thought, at more or less half that tale of years.

The small room filled with the smell of spice. Lionel produced soup plates, bowls and spoons and (of course he would) linen napkins, and distributed them on the table by the window.

'Would you care to give us a grace?' said Lionel unexpectedly. 'I saw so much starvation in the East, I've said grace ever since.'

'. . . this food to our use and ourselves to Thy service,' Theodora murmured. 'Where were you in the East?' she asked.

Lionel expertly shared the spiced duck in its thick red sauce between them and passed the bread.

'I had a ghastly eighteen months training bits of the Pakistani army just outside Dacca. I'd never seen poverty like it, even though I was born out in India just before the last war. My father was in the Indian Civil Service. The last batch before we left them to it. Actually, it wasn't so much the poverty which was so awful as the fact that there was an immense amount of conspicuous wealth right next to it. No one seemed to think it obscene except tourists like us.'

'I spent a couple of years in a first curacy in Nairobi and there was a fair amount there, but then everyone was poor, more or less, so it didn't bite so much. Did you enjoy your soldiering?'

'Yes, actually I did. I wasn't a success. I did fourteen years and came out a captain so you can judge I wasn't a high flyer. But I liked the variety, I liked seeing bits of the world, I even liked mess life. If you do like it, it's remarkably undemanding. You don't have to make a lot of effort. The rules are plain, the duties likewise. I suppose in a way it leaves you lazy and ill fitted for civilian life.'

'What did you do when you came out?'

'My father died and I went down to Dorset to see if I could be a farmer.'

'And?'

'Well, I couldn't. I made a disastrous land deal, we over-stretched and I went as near bankrupt as dammit. After that I went as an agent to an estate run by a consortium. A lot of sharks who really did only want profits and made a chemical sewer of the soil. There were days I felt physically sick. After that I did a bit of prep school teaching. I quite enjoyed it but it's repetitious. You find yourself making the same jokes at the same time of the term every year. You can get away with it because it's a different set of boys. But it atrophies the mind ultimately so then I came here, to serve the Church. Not much of a career.'

How very dull it sounded, Theodora thought, like a *Telegraph* obituary of solid middle-class failure. And yet she didn't feel Lionel to be a failure. He had spark, principle, an inner self-sufficiency which prohibited pity.

'But you're not a failure,' Theodora said before she'd had time to weigh her words.

Lionel grinned. 'Failure's in the mind, surely. It can't be how much money or even successful enterprises.'

'And the Church is worth our efforts?'

'As a worldly institution? Hardly. I feel all the zeal of my missionary ancestors when I think about it. It needs converting.'

Theodora laughed. 'To what?'

'To Christianity, which at the senior level it does not begin to attain. And lower down it could do with some basic business practices which could free its people to serve the world more effectively.'

'I sometimes feel it's hampered by its worldly role. It handles property badly,' Theodora agreed. 'Perhaps the Franciscan model might serve us better. Own nothing.'

Lionel snorted. 'Never prise the top clergy from their little bits of power.' He wiped his bread round his plate and served rice. 'Which brings us,' he said, 'back to the tricky question of the death of Mick Lee, the beating up of Leslie Wale, the putative blackmail of the Provost. Let's take it in order. What do we need to know?'

'Well, I haven't been too successful in tracking down Reggie's blackmailer, if indeed he is being blackmailed.'

'We could do with knowing more about who holds the title to the land over which the hypermarket wants its road.'

'So that would mean tracking down the surviving Lee.'

'Then we need to know much more about Wale Holdings.'

'Tricky.'

'Well, I don't know. The chair of the farming consortium I worked for might know something. He's a shark of about the same size as I judge Leslie Wale to be. And there's always Leslie himself.'

'He didn't look in too talkative a mode last night.'

'Still, I think one of us might do a bit of work on him, perhaps through Kate.' Lionel gazed meaningfully at Theodora.

'What are the police doing in all this?' Theodora asked. 'Where is your Inspector Spurt?'

'He's doing what police do best,' Lionel answered, 'he's trying to map everything which happened on the scaffolding site from the delivery of the wood on Thursday evening to Mick Lee's fall on Friday afternoon.'

'So what's he found?'

'In detail, of course, he won't tell me. But unless he's very lucky it's not going to be productive. The site is open, anyone could have got to the planks. He's checking traffic and following up dog-walkers and comparing the statements of the other brickies. He's either going to find that all of them could have done it or none of them could have.'

'He'd do better to approach it from the point of view of motive.'

'Like us.'

'Right. So the first thing is land ownership.'

'How about Father Angel? Might he know something about land ownership? Vince seemed to think—'

'I'll take Father Angel,' Theodora said firmly lest worse should befall her.

'Are you sure?' Lionel was solicitous. 'He's not that keen on women.'

'Then I'll be good practice for him.'

'OK. I'll try and make contact with the Lees, then we'll compare notes and see where we go after that.'

CHAPTER SEVEN: LEARNING

On Monday morning, St Sylvester and St Andrew's CE-Aided Primary School was more difficult to get into than Fordingham. It had a low fence round it and pretty cut-outs of trees on the windows which, in the nineteenth-century fashion, were set high in solid brick walls so that pupils couldn't look out of them. It abutted the nineteenth-century church of St Sylvester's but there was no sign of Father Tobias. It wasn't clear to Lionel which bit of the wicket perimeter fence gave way into being a gate. Minute examination revealed a padlock attached to part of it but the padlock turned out to be locked. In the end he discovered a gap through which he was able to edge. From there, gay yellow footsteps painted on the tarmac of the playground took over, leading him round the side of the building and up a wall.

Lionel halted. He knew he couldn't walk up walls. He looked closely. At the end of the trail of footsteps was a smiley face also painted in yellow below a notice which said, in a sudden leap into adult concepts, 'Reception'. The arrow pointed round the next side of the building. The door when reached said 'Welcome to St Sylvester and St Andrew's CE-Aided Primary School' in nice Microsoft 24-point Times New Roman alternating red and black letters along the inside of the glass.

Still there was no way through. There were a couple of new-looking locks and an entry phone which said in faded handwriting below it: 'Please speak here.' Lionel pressed the bell and waited for some considerable time. There was a clunking noise as the entry phone cleared its throat. Then a calm male voice said: 'Orlando Groom, headteacher, here. Please state your name and business.' Lionel had that one prepared. 'Lionel Comfet, Giltchrist Diocesan Office, message from one of your governors, Mrs Susan Tye.'

The door buzzed and, before it had time to recant, Lionel pushed his way in. He felt a sense of achievement.

It was some time, he realized, since he'd been in a primary school. Did they make all the pupils do that, he wondered. Nothing like a bit of obstruction for bringing out youngsters' mettle and making them value their education. He stood in the entrance hall. Tanks of fish, rubber plants, a couple of shelves of picture books, a frieze of dinosaurs and a plastic skeleton of the human frame were all neatly arranged round a low table with one or two infant-sized chairs which did not invite him to sit down. On the wall hung a wooden cross flanked by two modern ikons, one of St Sylvester, one of St Andrew.

'Never a dull moment,' said a cheerful voice behind him. 'Orlando Groom,' said the voice's owner, grey-haired but seeming younger than his hair. His tread was springy, his physical movements, like those of a gymnast, as though he might at any minute spring on to his hands and juggle a ball with his feet.

'Lionel Comfet,' said Lionel. 'I've come from Mrs Tye. She rang. The Lee child.'

'Right. Sad business.'

'Terrible.'

'How's he coping?'

'He did come in today. I thought perhaps he might not. In view of the circumstances. To be honest they're not great attenders at the best of times, though Henry Lee is better than some of his family. His grandmother looks after him and she doesn't want him under her feet so she walks him round here on average three days a week. His aunt collects him with her two.'

'How's Henry taking it?'

'Well, he's not a great talker ever. Oracy skill, National Curriculum English level two which isn't,' Orlando explained professionally, 'terribly good for year five. Narrowed vocabulary, rather few syntactical forms but good descriptive skills on how to skin a rabbit. Gets quite eloquent there.'

Lionel nodded. 'Mrs Tye seemed to think there ought to be some sort of act of worship or remembrance for Mick Lee. Yes?'

'We're working on it. It's not too easy. We mostly go on the supposition they're either actual or residual Christians but in Henry Lee's case I do rather wonder if that's not insulting.'

'Pagan?'

'Well, discernibly different. I mean, have you met the grandmother or the aunt?'

Lionel shook his head.

'I wouldn't be surprised if they didn't do something at the full moon. Possibly with rabbit's blood. Let's hope so. I mean, let's hope it's rabbit's.'

'A violent family?' Lionel hazarded.

'Values certainly differ here. Cray Martyr on the one hand, Gainshurst on the other. It's a mixed catchment, as we say.'

Orlando Groom was embarked on his special subject. Lionel, always happy to extend his factual knowledge, settled down to map the culture.

'It's a question of what you think of as success. The Gainshurst lot want their kids to pass the county selective test to go on to the remaining grammar schools. The Cray Martyr ones don't. In fact apart from one or two families they'd really rather not have anything to do with education at all.'

'Makes for a difficult culture,' Lionel agreed.

But Orlando was launched. 'You see,' he went on, 'the Cray Martyr lot can get as far as the dinosaurs but computerized pie charts leave them cold.'

'Motivation,' Lionel suggested.

'Exactly. Gainshurst has it for what it thinks is education. Cray Martyr hasn't got it for what it thinks is education.'

'Both wrong about education.' Lionel was enjoying himself.

'Oh, yes. "The best that has been thought and said and done,"' Orlando quoted with relish. 'That's gone out with the National Curriculum. We have to beggar about with an awful lot of science and maths. It's quite disproportionate.'

'What's happened to history?'

'You may well ask. It lost out to geography,' said Orlando grimly. 'More scientific, supposedly. Romans and Tudors through artefacts is about as much as we're allowed. It's called humanities but it's not humane. We've got very concrete, lost out on ideas. Theory is, it makes people easier to manipulate if they don't know any history.'

'How do you manage?' Lionel was curious.

'With difficulty. We have to juggle.' Lionel thought he really was going to spring on to his hands. 'But are we downhearted? No. I like the challenge. You don't want to be a governor by any chance?'

Lionel looked startled.

'No, well, I can't say I blame you. Though it's very worthwhile work. We're always on the lookout for new talent.'

'I haven't got any talents,' said Lionel. 'I never did have. I'm happy to say that I have failed at whatever I have undertaken. I'm about to retire and I thought I might make a success of that. It would make a change.'

'You sound as though you might have much to offer,' said Orlando thoughtfully. 'We can use recent retirees. People have a shelf-life. Once they're more than five years removed they tend to lose their short-term memory and hark back to their heyday twenty years before.'

'Talk of "when I was a lad".'

'Right. We've got rather too many of those at the moment. I'm looking for a counterweight.'

'Susan Tye's quite young.'

'Yes, and I wouldn't be without her.' Orlando was loyal. 'But she hasn't got youngsters here and she's a bit inclined to want to recruit poor mathematics specialists on the grounds that they're sound Christians.'

'Perverse.'

'Not ultimately, of course. But given the demands of the National Curriculum, yes.'

'Look here,' said Lionel, suddenly moved with the thought of a new career, 'I can read a balance sheet. Say I give it a go and promise never to hark back to when I was a lad.'

'That's very sporting of you. How about coming along this evening for a preview? There's a meeting at seven. If you like it, I'll get the Archdeacon to put you on as diocesan nominee. How about it?'

Lionel saw a whole new life opening before him. 'Done,' he said amiably.

'Excellent,' said Groom. 'I'll fix it with our chair. Do you know him? Tobias Angel. He's vicar of St Sylvester's. Bit of a card but means well. Sometimes a bit difficult to get hold of in an emergency. Keeps odd hours.'

And has odd jobs, Lionel thought, recalling his brother's remarks.

'Does a prison chaplaincy job too, doesn't he?'

'Yes. Fordingham. We took the fifth years to do a Christmas pantomime there, year before last. It was a great success. An eye-opener for the kids. The Gainshurst crew who thought prison was all slammed doors and dungeons. The Cray Martyr crew who thought all prisons were crammed with their relations when in fact they were full of upper-class rogues. You know, it's really quite civilized. I could do a spell of rest there.'

'Only, you can't leave when you want,' said Lionel.

'No, I suppose there is that. Look, if it's the Lee women you want, you can see one of them, the aunt, when we finish. Four minutes. She collects her two from years one and three.'

Even as he spoke a small boy dashed past them through the hall and made for a switch high up beside one of the ikons. A light, high bell sounded the first two bars of 'Ode to Joy' in a key for which it was not written.

'Thank you very much, Robert,' said Orlando. Robert took no notice and shot out towards the cloakroom.

'We practise positive discipline here,' Orlando said by way of explanation, though whether of his own or the boy's conduct Lionel was not sure. A whole new vocabulary awaits me, he thought happily.

'If you'd care to come into my office you can have a look at Mrs Lee from a safe distance and see if you want to see her.'

'What happened to the other Mrs Lee, Henry's mother, Mick's wife?' Lionel asked.

'Left soon after Henry was born.'

Lionel edged into a room the size of a cupboard with a bank of computers, printers, faxes, photocopiers and answering machines. A couple of music stands and a keyboard rested against a drum set.

'They don't design primary schools with enough storage space. And, of course, computers take more space than pen and ink.'

Lionel picked his way to the window and peered out.

The school fence was now reinforced by a solid phalanx of women. Many had other, smaller children attached to them by hand, pushchair or miniature mountain bike. Some had dogs winding leads round wheels. Beyond the ring of women could be seen a line of parked cars.

'Volvos, Suzukis, four-wheel drives and the odd BMW are Gainshurst. Cray Martyr,' Orlando gestured towards the other end, 'runs to very big Fords or else they come on foot. That's young Mrs Lee nearest the gate. No one disputes her place.'

Lionel saw a small thin figure in a pink leather miniskirt and black short-sleeved top. Her hair was very black and reached her bare shoulders. She had long gilt earrings but her face, narrow with long frown lines on the brow, was devoid of make-up.

'Could be auditioning for Carmen,' Lionel said.

'I never thought of that,' said the resourceful head-teacher. 'It's a possibility. We do a parents' show in the summer term to raise funds for the computers. Wonder what her voice is like.'

'But in the circumstances — her brother-in-law's death and so on,' Lionel said.

'Oh, quite,' Orlando agreed professionally and very fast. 'Still, life must go on. Time the great healer. And computers always need updating.'

Lionel manoeuvred himself towards the door. 'I think I must at least try to have a word with her, for propriety's sake.' Had Orlando heard of propriety, Lionel wondered as he moved into the playground.

Mrs Lee clutched her youngest to her breast and looked at Lionel as though he hadn't spoken English or, perhaps, she understood none. Lionel thought for a moment that she might cut him. She had such an air of tenseness and unused and unusable energy about her that Lionel felt pity.

'Mrs Lee,' he began, 'we wanted . . . that is, the diocesan office wanted . . . the Church . . .' He wished he had the courage to say what he thought, to say it in his own person.

Mrs Lee leaned away from him and shouted over the low fence. 'Tara, Shaun, over here. And bring Henry with you.'

Two dark-haired youngsters, male and female, but not easily distinguished, ran across the playground dragging a short, stockier boy between them.

'Mrs Lee, I was so sorry about your brother-in-law. I knew him.'

Mrs Lee stopped short in the course of gathering her family. She gave him no eye contact but looked over his head and said with great intensity, 'How'd you know him? He never did know you.'

She seemed to find the idea an insult.

'I used to watch him. I saw him every morning. We both used to come in early. He to the building site, me to the office.'

'He never should have gone and worked for them. Watch him. What for? Why'd you watch him?'

'I admired his dexterity.' Lionel sorted through his vocabulary. 'He was nimble and,' he added, 'courageous.'

This she could manage. 'He never felt fear,' she agreed. 'He'd go up and up.'

'If there's any help . . . support we . . . the Church can give.'

She seemed to refocus on him. 'The Church? We need money.'

'I think the employers' insurers will be looking to that side of things. I meant prayer or someone to talk to.'

'Ha! Prayer. I pray they'll rot in hell, them who killed him. We know about them. They're dead.' She looked Lionel full in the face. 'You can tell them that.'

* * *

Reggie seemed to have conquered his surprise at seeing his wife's guest round the house. Indeed, it was Susan who regarded him with amazement as he lurched into the kitchen at twelve thirty for lunch on Monday.

'I thought you said you were lunching with Marcus More.'

Reggie looked surprised. 'Marcus More,' he repeated as though the name were unfamiliar to him.

'You did say so. You did, Reggie, on Friday when I told you about picking Theo up and we arranged about eating for this week, you said you wouldn't be in to lunch on Monday. You remember. Now run along, there's nothing for you here.'

Did Reggie behave childishly because Susan treated him like a child or did she treat him like a child because he behaved childishly, Theodora wondered. Reggie's lip puckered and Theodora thought he might burst into tears. However, he roused himself like a man and said heroically, 'Oh, right. I might just catch him. I'll just . . . just.' He swung himself round the edge of the table and clambered over the pile of curtains beside the door. The spaniel regarded him with compassion.

As soon as Reggie had left, Susan sprang into action. She produced the chunk of cheese which had last appeared at Friday evening's supper, likewise the bread and a jar of pickle with rather little in the bottom. 'Now,' she said, turning to Theodora, 'we need to pool information and get a plan together.'

'What about?' Theodora was stubborn. She took the opportunity to get a stab at the cheese while this was still possible.

Susan ignored the provocation. 'You tell me about the Vincent thing and I'll tell you what I've learned about Mick Lee. Then we take some action against Reggie's troublemaker. So,' her hostess leaned across the table and gazed earnestly into Theodora's face, 'shoot.'

Theodora paused to consider whether the source of Susan's diction was Chandler or old TV films. She also wondered how much she was prepared to tell her about the information gleaned at Fordingham. Ought she not to consult Lionel, ask his leave, before she divulged facts about his brother?

However, at last she said, 'There are a number of strands.' This seemed safe and true.

Susan was not impressed. She moved the cheese nearer to her own plate and cut a minute sliver. She did not move it back into the common ground on the table between the two of them where it would have been decent for Theodora to reach for a refill. 'Such as?'

'Vincent Comfet told us that Leslie Wale used him as his agent to negotiate a land deal with the Lees.'

'What land deal?'

'Have you heard of Mackenzie's All Foods?'

'MAF, yes. In fact they've cropped up somewhere else recently.' Susan wrinkled her nose as others might their brows. 'Go on.'

'MAF want to build a hypermarket on the land at the back of the church, St Sylvester's. And they'd have to build an access road across a bit of land which the Lees own.'

'Why did MAF use Wale Holdings and why did Wale Holdings use Vincent Comfet?'

'Vincent thinks MAF wanted to stay in the background because if it were known that they were the principals the price from the Lees would have escalated. Wale Holdings has shares in MAF. Vincent was a local boy with only a small practice so he'd evoke no suspicion. And Wale used Vincent because Wale himself had a previous run-in with the Lees about the land for a bypass.'

'So what next?'

Theodora thought how best to put this. 'Vincent's theory is that the land title itself may not be too secure. It might be difficult for either the Lees or the Church to prove a title.'

'Who knows who owns the land?'

Theodora admired Susan's grasp.

'I mean,' Susan went on, 'we need to know about that first. Then we need to know who else would know how to find out about it.' Susan looked expectantly at Theodora. Theodora reckoned she'd earned a reward and gestured towards the cheese. Susan pushed it a short way towards her.

'It's often not too easy. The diocesan registrar should have deeds or records but sometimes they don't have them all. Sometimes they're still in the hands of the incumbent or even in the hands of the long-serving members of the PCC. I remember when Uncle Hugh was Archdeacon of Medewich he practically had to go to war with an old boy who'd been on the PCC for fifty-two years and seemed to regard the deeds to some of their church's land as his personal property. In fact when he died he'd arranged for them to be buried with him. Indecorous scenes at the burial while Uncle stopped the funeral to have them torn from his coffin.'

'Go on,' said Susan, genuinely interested. 'So where do we start?'

'In a well-run diocesan office they ought to have a list of where they're all to be found.'

Susan looked doubtful. 'I'm not too sure whether ours is a well-run office,' she admitted at last. 'I believe I've heard

Lionel say it's, well . . . a shambles. Still,' she went on, 'perhaps we ought to try. Or,' she had a flash of inspiration, 'there's Reggie's study. Would he have a list or anything?'

'It's not strictly cathedral business, but I suppose he might have. Who's the patron of the living? I mean, if the Provost and Chapter are . . .'

'Ah, that I do know. I'm a governor of the school next door, St Sylvester and St Andrew's, and the trustees for the school site are the same as the trustees for the land the church is built on. And the patrons are the trustees. It's the Foundation of St Sylvester. I don't suppose you've—'

'Yes I have,' said Theodora brusquely. 'I'm curate of one of their churches.'

'Oh, yes, of course you are. St Sylvester's Betterhouse. I'm so sorry, I wasn't thinking.'

Theodora reflected on how little interest others take in what is of first importance in our own lives. Here she was giving her total attention to Susan and her worries and Susan clearly neither knew nor cared about her, Theodora's, life.

'Come on,' Susan said, taking the cheese from the table and placing it back in the fridge. 'Let's have a peek at Reggie's room while he's still out and see what we can find.'

Reggie's room, like the rest of the house, had the air of temporary and incomplete habitation. It was a large room on the ground floor. Only part of it was occupied by Reggie. He'd opted for a desk by the window. There was a single chair. One of its legs was very neatly bound up with string. Although the October afternoon was bright, the room was in half-darkness, the blind halfway down the single window. Its acorn gently tapped against the window pane for the top half of the window was open and admitted a slight breeze.

'We really ought to get to grips with this one,' Susan said with energy. 'And look.' She gestured to the far end of the room. 'There are some deed boxes here. Odd I never noticed them.' Against the empty bookshelves were stacked four black tin boxes. They had the names of parishes stamped on them in white paint. Theodora bent down to read the names. The final one said 'St Sylvester Cray Martyr'.

'Open it,' said Susan quietly.

Theodora raised the lid. Inside were two documents, both with seals, one folded, one rolled. Theodora took them out and brought them over to the desk to make use of the light. Carefully she spread them out. The copperplate of the 1860s was beautiful, flowing, self-assured. No fancy computer face rivalled it.

'Well?' Susan asked.

Theodora shook her head. 'Neither of these relates to any land except the site of the church and the school adjacent to it. The school one is a conveyance document rather than an actual trust deed though it does talk about "a place of learning for the poor of Cray Martyr" and "their instruction in the faith of the Church of England".'

'What about the other one?'

'As I say, nothing about land other than that on which the church is built. What we're looking for is the title to the land between the church and Cray Common. That's the Lees' land.'

Susan was deflated. 'We'll have to go and see what we can find in the diocesan office, then.'

Having come thus far Theodora could see no way out. She rolled the deed which had been rolled and folded the one which had been folded and put them back in their box. Reggie's desk was as dusty as the deeds. The single sheet of recently used paper headed 'Cathedral Restoration Funding' suggested his present preoccupation. Theodora's eye swept the list. Then she stopped. 'Mackenzie's All Foods.' And beside it, she counted the noughts, one million pounds. She opened her mouth to speak and then shut it again.

'Come on,' said Susan. 'Next stop the office.'

'And after that,' Theodora said, 'I think perhaps I ought to see Father Angel.'

* * *

Mrs Lure liked a long lunch hour but did not always choose to leave the office in order to take it. She put up the 'Gone to lunch' sign on her door sharp on twelve thirty and did not expect to turn it round until two. Then she brought out her packet of dainty, almost crocheted, sandwiches and home-baked biscuits and spread them out on her desk amongst the crumbs of the previous day's meal.

She had dusted the rubber plant and placed *The British Needlewoman* athwart the keyboard of her computer. She was not pleased, therefore, to hear the voices of two women ascending the stairs. On the other hand she had no reason to suppose they would dare to intrude.

Theodora halted at the top of the stairs. 'Why don't we wait until Lionel gets back and ask him? He ought to know.'

'He could be ages. I asked him to go down to Cray Martyr, to the school, to enquire about the Lee boy. And he said he wanted to see if he could make contact with Mrs Lee. Surely it ought to be obvious if there is a list of land holdings and surely there ought to be no secret about who owns what.'

'It's amazing what the Church thinks it can and ought to keep secret,' said Theodora, no novice in this area. Privately she had her own agenda. What she needed was confirmation of the amazing list she'd just looked at in Reggie's study. A list of the Friends of the Cathedral and a copy of their accounts would be a start.

'Actually,' Susan was pressing on, 'we don't need the whole list of land ownership. All we're really looking for is the St Sylvester's stuff.' Susan turned through ninety degrees like a beagle on a scent and made for Mrs Lure's door.

'You know, the people who always know about these sorts of things are the secretaries. I wonder if Mrs Lure's in?' Susan swung across the landing and opened the door. 'Mrs Lure, how absolutely amazing. We were just saying you knew everything about everybody and you are just the person we want.'

Mrs Lure put down her sandwich with deliberation. 'Mrs Tye,' she said and then to mark the degree of relationship, 'Susan. I am actually just about to start my very precious lunch hour.' She smiled her glassy smile. 'Quality time is so very important in a stressful office environment.'

'Oh, absolutely,' Susan agreed. 'We wouldn't dream of disturbing you.' She gazed with disapproval at the frugal round of sandwiches. 'It's only a matter of pointing us in the right direction. You're bound to know. And Miss Braithwaite here has such a short time with us. We have to make the most. Miss Braithwaite,' Susan lied with aplomb, Theodora noticed, 'is a church historian and she's interested in St Sylvester's because she's a curate at another St Sylvester's foundation in Betterhouse. I expect you've heard of it.'

Mrs Lure was non-committal.

'What she would really like to do is look at the ancient records, the title deeds and so on, for our St Sylvester's. Now where would we find them?'

Mrs Lure could hardly believe her ears. Her smile was basilisk-like but she was smart enough to realize that she had met her match in Susan. She made her wait, however. 'St Sylvester's, now.' She hummed and appeared to go off into a reverie. Finally, 'It could be . . .'

'Yes?' said Susan.

'It could be that their stuff is in the archive room.'

'Yes?' said Susan to keep things bowling along.

'You'll need a key,' Mrs Lure paused and then added, 'and of course you really ought to have permission from the diocesan secretary.'

They both laughed merrily at this to show that Susan wasn't going to bother about this and Mrs Lure wasn't in any position to insist.

'The key,' said Mrs Lure to show who was in control, 'is here.'

She opened a drawer in her desk, produced a bunch of keys of great diversity and detached one of the largest. 'First door on your right at the end of the corridor.' She held up a minatory finger and wagged it at Theodora. 'I'm sure you'll leave things just as you find them. One collection misplaced and it's lost for all eternity.'

'Surely not,' murmured Theodora.

'You'd be surprised.'

They scampered down the corridor just as years ago they had scampered down school corridors after being released from class. Mrs Lure had that effect on people. The archive room door was fireproof and heavy. It yielded to the key and together they edged inside. There was no natural light and for a moment they could not find the switch, then Theodora reached up and put her hand on it, high up on the wall above the door. They expected anyone using the room to be at least six foot one and able to see in the dark. A single sixty-watt bulb cast its anaemic illumination over shelves of staging reaching to the ceiling. A narrow passage ran down the middle.

'Will there be any system, that is the question,' Susan said.

There was a system. It was geographical by deanery. It took them some time to work this out and had not Theodora been wise in the arcane thought-forms of diocesan administration they might never have cracked it. The records were kept in cardboard spring box files, sometimes several to a parish, or, where there had been a shortage of these sophisticated bits of office equipment, simply wrapped in blue cardboard covers. This time it involved squatting on the floor. Susan ticked off the parishes in the deanery of Gainshurst, reciting them like a litany. 'St Martin Ever Tourney, St Saviour Little Bradlaugh, St Mary and St Margaret Berrington, St Andrew Gainshurst, St Sylvester Cray Martyr.' She stopped short. 'There's nothing here,' she wailed.

Theodora edged in beside her. It was true. The label on the shelf proclaimed the parish but above it was a gap. Theodora looked carefully at the dust. 'It's been gone some time.'

'Oh, you're so clever.' Susan was not ironical. 'So who took it, and why?'

'The Venerable Marcus More on the twenty-fifth of June,' Theodora answered crisply. Susan's admiration knew no bounds. Theodora held up the slip of paper poked into the gap and bearing the Archdeacon's name. 'Why he took it three months ago, I wouldn't know. There may be a perfectly innocent administrative reason for his wanting it.'

'A likely tale,' Susan snorted. 'Here we have a church which has possibly a valuable piece of land next to it, which may in fact have a claim on that land, and the file goes missing!' Susan wrung the drama from the situation.

'It hasn't gone missing. We know exactly where it is,' Theodora objected.

'So we must go in hot pursuit,' Susan said.

* * *

The Venerable Marcus More's house was in the fashionable part of the town, as Lionel had said, at the opposite end of Giltchrist to his own digs. Because Giltchrist was a modern cathedral it had not run to a full complement of dignitaries' lodgings round a close. The Provost's Lodging, the Bishop's Palace, the diocesan office and a rehearsal room for the choir were all that Maufe's pupil had money for. A precentor, an organist and the diocesan secretary, therefore, had diocesan houses scattered round Giltchrist, maintaining the architectural presence of the cathedral's red brick and white stone coping in quite other contexts. Of these the diocesan secretary's was by far the grandest. It had well-grown privet hedges on four sides and, inside the hedge, lawns and beds planted with dahlias and begonias. If it was possible for a garden to be ugly, Theodora thought, this one achieved it.

'We could have rung him,' she objected to Susan as they pulled up in front of the house.

'Have you no sense of urgency?' Susan panted as she banged the door of the ten-year-old Nissan.

Theodora thought of the way in which her precious holiday time had been eaten up by Susan's affairs over the last four days and felt this was unfair.

The doorbell in the mock Georgian porch was one of the chime variety. It failed to express Susan's feelings so she kept her finger on it. It refused to do more than a demure repetition.

The man who opened the door was unshaven and had a towel in his hand with which he was failing to staunch a flow of blood from his index finger. He wore a striped football shirt and denims stained with sump oil. He looked about twelve going on twenty-five. Limp, fair hair drooped over his brow. He gazed with distaste at the pair in front of him.

Susan beamed an immense smile at him. 'Tony, how very nice to see you. Are you well? Your poor finger. Is your father in?'

The youth did not bother with the niceties of replying. He switched the bloody tea towel over his shoulder and shouted up the staircase behind him. 'Dad? Mrs Tye to see you.'

Susan recognized there would be no point in waiting to be invited in and walked into the hall. It smelt of dust and bleach.

'The son is a great disappointment to Marcus,' Susan whispered to Theodora not *sotto voce* enough. 'He can't hold a job down. Spends his entire time underneath old cars. I expect he'll go into the Church in the end.'

Theodora nodded and expected he would. The wait went on. Susan took to clearing her throat in a meaningful manner. Eventually a door opened at the top of the stairs and the Venerable Marcus More descended. His tall concave figure dominated the hall. He could not have been described as being overjoyed to see them. He seemed at a loss to know what to do with them.

'Marcus,' said Susan. 'I don't think you've met Miss Braithwaite, an old school chum of mine.'

The Archdeacon contained his enthusiasm.

'Theodora's a great church historian and she's also a curate at St Sylvester's Betterhouse, a brother, or should it be a sister, house to our St Sylvester at Cray Martyr.'

At the mention of the church's name Marcus More decided that this wasn't something he was going to be able to avoid altogether. 'Shall we go into my study?' he said. 'There's more privacy there.'

Odd that privacy should be his first concern, Theodora reflected, as they followed his lean back through the hall and into a large room with a view of the privets and dahlias. Certainly relaxation was not his aim. Why do the clergy live so uncomfortably, Theodora wondered. Was it a penance for all the beauty with which they were quite often surrounded? Or was it a sense of guilt that they had things which lined them up with the middle classes and which the poor, to whom the Gospel professionally committed them, did not have? Even her own dear father had no instinct for making himself comfortable. This room was full of battered and scratched reproduction furniture dating from the 1930s. It looked as though generations of very destructive children had jabbed their pencils into the French polish and hacked at the peeling veneer with penknives.

'Tea?' queried the Archdeacon as they gingerly placed themselves on a sofa whose springs were visible through its thin beige damask.

'That's awfully kind of you, Marcus.' Susan was clearly going to do the talking. 'But we really don't have time. We're working against the clock.'

Which clock would that be, wondered Theodora, who would have liked tea.

Marcus looked relieved and sat down behind his desk. The authoritative position restored him to his usual manner. 'I quite understand. I'm up to my eyes.' He tapped the diary on the desk and looked at his watch. 'I'm extremely sorry but I can't spare you more than a few minutes.'

'Oh, I do so understand.' Susan could not have been more understanding. Theodora was beginning to admire her friend's talents. She certainly knew the senior clergy's little ways.

'It's really quite simple. Theodora's looking at the St Sylvester foundations all over the country.'

'All four of them,' Theodora intervened. She thought really one should be economical with one's lies.

'All of them,' Susan said firmly. 'And, of course, she wants to see our one in its context. Land ownership, history of its churchmanship. That sort of thing. So naturally I thought of you, as Archdeacon. And diocesan secretary. Concerned with every one of our parish churches.' Susan hammered it home.

'Of course history's not my area. I really don't know that I can be of any help.' It went against the grain for Marcus More to admit that there was something he didn't know. But looking at Theodora he had the intuition that just following his usual practice of making it up might not work.

'But the site's a terribly interesting one, isn't it?'

'How do you mean?' More was cautious.

'In the green belt with odd bits of adjacent land given to it by . . .' Susan turned to Theodora for confirmation.

'Thomas Henry Newcome, our founder,' Theodora supplied.

'Thomas Henry Newcome.' Susan appropriated the name.

'Yes, er, well, but . . .'

'You must know something.' Susan switched to the direct mode. 'You've got the historical stuff from the diocesan archive.'

A slow flush suffused Marcus More's face, joining up the pink patches which were there more permanently. He took refuge in the Church's favourite ploy. 'The archive material is confidential.'

'Oh, surely not.' Theodora lent a hand. 'Most of the material either is or ought to be in the public records department or the land register.' She saw no reason to tell him how flawed these were as sources of information and how valuable therefore the diocesan records could be.

'I referred to the fact that I have not advertised that it was I who withdrew the material from the office archive.'

Susan gave a good imitation of amazement. Or was it an imitation, Theodora wondered. She couldn't help feeling that her friend was revealing more talent for this sort of thing than she might have supposed. 'Surely there's no reason for secrecy,' Susan said.

'It would be very interesting to have those documents on your St Sylvester's even if you could spare them for only a short time,' Theodora contributed.

For a moment they both thought that More was going to refuse outright. 'Say, just for tonight,' Susan wheedled.

Maybe More thought that they would go on sitting there and arguing the toss until he gave in or maybe he was just too surprised to withstand the dual attack further.

'Well, of course, we must put the claims of scholarship high on our list of priorities.'

He narrowed the corners of his eyes in what was sometimes mistaken, by those who did not know him, for a smile. He opened one of the desk drawers and took out a large bundle of material wrapped in brown paper.

'If I could have them back here, on my desk,' he tapped it, 'within twenty-four hours, without fail.'

For the second time in the afternoon Theodora felt she was being treated like a pupil. But Susan lost no time. 'How very very kind of you, Marcus.' She smiled at him. 'Of course we'll be very, very careful of them and you shall have them back as soon as may be.'

CHAPTER EIGHT: INTERVIEWING

The headline of the *Giltchrist Telegraph* ran LOCAL FAMILY: TRAGEDY STRIKES AGAIN. Under it was a report on the death of Mick Lee who had fallen from scaffolding while working on the restoration of Giltchrist Cathedral. It pointed out that the family had suffered an earlier bereavement when a younger brother had been the victim of a hit and run car accident three years ago. Lionel winced at the inaccuracy.

The paper was spread out on Lionel's office desk. The office had that peace which falls upon workplaces when the workers have gone home, a sort of slumbering complacency. The raft of typists and assistants on the ground floor had departed on the stroke of five from the cathedral clock. Mrs Lure had sailed down the stairs a minute later. None of them would think of their work for another sixteen hours. Through the window the late afternoon sun caught the bright brick spire. No work was proceeding.

Theodora had placed the trophies won from the Archdeacon on the table. For the last half-hour they had studied the slim bundle of papers together. It was to be a sharing of information. Susan had gone home to 'do something towards Reggie's supper, poor man. I mustn't neglect him.' Theodora wondered what preparations she had in mind. Cheese salad had been indicated as a possible menu.

Underneath the newspaper story was a picture of the three Lee brothers taken a while ago. In the middle was the oldest and surviving brother Deke, to his left was Vincent's victim Jon and on his other hand was Mick. In front of them was a sheet with the words 'Our homes, Your countryside, Their road' painted on it.

'And that was the previous plan for the bypass,' Theodora said.

'Right. As projected it would have taken out a fair number of council and private properties in Cray Martyr,' Lionel replied.

'Including the Lees'?'

'Oh, yes. Slap bang in the middle.'

'But it never happened?'

'It seemed to go away in the end.'

'The paper doesn't mention a police inquiry into Mick's death.'

'I noticed that,' Lionel agreed. 'I'm going to have another word with my ex-sergeant now inspector. We could do with knowing how far they've got.'

'Would he tell you that?'

'Comrades in arms, a great bond. He won't break confidences but he'll answer the sort of questions I'll want to put.'

'Such as?'

'Who they've questioned.'

'Ah,' said Theodora. She thought this was rather acute.

'In the light of what we have here,' Lionel tapped the bundle of St Sylvester's papers, 'it's clear that the strip of land bordering the back of the school and the church—'

'The land which would be needed for MAF's access road.'

'Right. Originally belonged to the church.'

'So where did Vincent get the idea that it belonged to the Lees?'

'The operative document is this.' Lionel leaned across the table and pushed the typewritten page towards Theodora. 'This says that the land was leased to Michael Lee in 1957.'

'Which Lee would that be?'

'About right for the grandfather of the three brothers, I'd guess.'

'What would he want it for?'

'He kept, indeed the Lees still keep, horses. And they also deal in scrap metal and car parts, that sort of line.'

'But if the Lees only rented it and the title still remained with the church, they couldn't sell it and they wouldn't get the profit from the sale.'

'On the other hand, if these documents are not complete and if the land was sold to the Lees after '57 . . .'

'They'd clean up,' Theodora concluded.

'So the point is,' Lionel pushed the papers across to her, 'are these the only documents?'

Theodora thought for a moment. 'I rather think not.'

'Evidence?'

'All the files in the archive room were either in box files or else in blue cardboard wrappers. This lot,' she indicated the bundle on Lionel's desk, 'are wrapped in new-looking brown paper.'

'So Marcus has still got some of them.'

'It's a possibility,' Theodora agreed. 'Though why do you think More wanted it?'

'Archdeacons and diocesan secretaries are supposed to keep an eye on land development, that sort of thing.'

'And the other interesting question is who else would know this? For instance, what made Vincent think the Lees had ownership?'

'He said, didn't he, that was what he was told by Wale?'

'How would Wale know?'

'Could the Lees have told him?'

'I thought that Wale was using Vincent because he wanted to conceal his interest from them.'

'It's a bit like playing chess, isn't it?' Lionel leaned back in his chair and regarded Theodora as though she might be an interesting opponent.

'So we need to see Wale then?'

Lionel nodded. 'And the other interesting question is why did Marcus More take out the file when he did?'

'He took it out in June,' Theodora pointed out. 'Why would he do that?'

'The Archdeacon stroke diocesan secretary is undoubtedly the idlest man I've ever worked with, for, or under. His whole object in life is to do as little as possible and then stop anyone else doing anything.'

'So, what you're saying is, he would have had to have had a really pressing reason to get the St Sylvester file out of the archive.'

'Yep. Normally he'd send me or Veronica Lure to get any files he wanted. It's beneath his dignity to walk down a corridor and pick a file off a shelf.'

'Mrs Lure didn't mention he'd been in the archive room. Would he need to ask her for a key?'

'No, as diocesan secretary he has his own set.'

'Have you got a set?' Theodora was direct.

'Heavens, no. I'm just the counterhand round here.'

'So if I hadn't wanted the file in my supposed historical research endeavours . . .'

'No one need have known he'd got it.'

'Why did he leave that marker slip with his name and date on it?'

'Given that no one except him and Mrs Lure could get in, it might be he felt there was no harm and perhaps he just wanted to mark the spot. There are an awful lot of files to get in a muddle if one wasn't careful.'

'What on earth could he have wanted it for? It must have been to do with the ownership of the land, mustn't it? I mean, that's all the file deals with. Do you suppose he could have got wind of MAF's interest in that bit of land?'

'He might have. The possibilities are, the Lees, who have no reason to tell him. Or Vincent, who didn't or else he would have told us. Or Wale who wanted to keep the whole thing quiet, presumably until he'd got the Lees to sell.'

'What about MAF?'

'What about them?'

'I mean,' said Theodora, 'who's head of the firm?'

'Man called Mackenzie. Let's have a look at him.' Lionel reached for *Who's Who* and flipped the pages. 'It's the grandson of Hector Mackenzie, I seem to remember. Ah, here we are. "Alexander Hector Mackenzie, born 1937, etc."' Lionel paused.

'Well?'

'Member of the Royal Company of Dry Victuallers.'

'Never heard of them,' said Theodora.

'Well, not perhaps quite in the first rank of livery companies, I grant you. But they have one interesting feature I happen to know about.' Lionel raised his eyes and grinned with real pleasure at Theodora. 'What could be more appropriate for one of the youngest livery companies than that one of the youngest cathedrals should provide its chaplain?'

'The Venerable Marcus More?'

'Wrong. The Very Reverend the Provost of Giltchrist.'

'Reggie!' exclaimed Theodora.

'The very same.'

Theodora digested this. Then she made a decision. She had to trust someone and there didn't seem to be anyone else with whom she could share this particular confidence. 'This afternoon,' she began, 'when we, Susan and I, were searching Reggie's room to see if he had any records of land ownership, I happened to glance at his desk.' Theodora felt uncomfortable about this sort of conduct.

Lionel recognized her scruple and nudged her gently forward. 'Difficult sometimes not to pick up the odd bit of information accidentally,' he reassured her.

'I happened to see a list of contributors to the cathedral restoration fund.'

Lionel caught her tone. It was going to be important.

'MAF figured. The contribution stood at one million pounds.'

'Hell's teeth,' said Lionel, genuinely shaken.

'Do you know anything about the restoration fund?'

'Well, it's very much Reggie's pigeon naturally, as Provost. It's the only thing I notice he puts himself out for. He's not been too successful to date. He doesn't nurse the Friends the way he should. I'm secretary to the fund committee. If Reggie has had a contribution from MAF of a million, I ought to have known about it.'

'Have you a list of contributors?'

'Reggie's never shown me one. I never imagined he'd be businesslike enough to have one.'

'How long has the fund been going?'

'He started it when he came about three years ago, as an offshoot of the Friends. But it hasn't gone anywhere until . . .' Lionel thought back. 'Until Friday, the day of Lee's death, Reggie suddenly announced that Sir Derek, what's his name, English Heritage, had told him that they'd match the fund pound for pound if they got a quarter of a million of their own together. And that if they didn't manage that, English Heritage weren't going to play. I think that was what Reggie was saying. The Lee thing interrupted the meeting and rather put it out of my mind.'

'How much have they got so far?'

'About twelve thousand.'

'So a contribution of a million from MAF would solve their problems.'

'More than somewhat,' Lionel agreed. 'But why should MAF give the cathedral restoration fund a million?'

'I imagine the usual mixed motives. Favourable publicity perhaps,' Theodora suggested.

'You can get good publicity a good deal cheaper than that.'

'Because Reggie and Mackenzie are fellow livery men?'

'I don't think enterprises like Mackenzie's All Foods are built up on sentiments like that.' Lionel was cynical.

'So what would the cathedral, what would Reggie, have to offer that MAF would want?'

It was clear to Lionel that Theodora could answer her own question. However, he pressed on. 'If the Church owned the land on which the access road for MAF's new superstore was going to be built and if the Church could guarantee good title to that land and were willing to sell . . .' Lionel left the equation in the air.

'But if on the other hand the Church did not have title to it, if it had sold it to the Lees some time in the fifties or indeed later . . .'

'Awkward. Loss of a million to a restoration fund,' Lionel agreed. 'Are we getting somewhere?'

'It's a bit hypothetical. How would it connect with Mick Lee's death, for example? You can't really suppose Reggie would kill a Lee to grab a million. Anyway, Reggie wouldn't know one end of a saw from another.'

'Two very different sorts of reason,' said Lionel philosophically. 'I suppose he might get someone else to do it.'

'He is such a bungler,' Theodora said. 'Wouldn't it be more likely that he let the thing about MAF's offer slip out by accident to Marcus?'

'You mean Marcus learned by accident and then made his own arrangements,' Lionel finished.

'He didn't strike me as much more capable than Reggie when we met him this afternoon.'

Lionel considered this. 'You saw him on his home ground where he's not at his sharpest. He's got a sick wife. Mildred's got over cancer twice but isn't a well woman. And his son . . .'

'Can't hold a job down,' Theodora finished. 'Susan did mention it.'

'In his work he's quite able to add two and two. In that respect he's much sharper than Reggie. No contest. But he never wants to do anything. He's . . .' Lionel searched for the words. 'He's dilatory and costive.'

'Worst case scenario,' said Theodora, summarizing, 'Reggie wants a million from MAF and can get it if the Church can prove title to access land which MAF needs for its road. Reggie not too sure about land title and tries to check it. But—'

'Either before he can do that, or perhaps because he doesn't know which way's up, he lets Marcus More know about it.'

'Marcus realizes that the Church hasn't got title but the Lees have.'

'Would Marcus More think a million for a cathedral was worth a life?'

'It's like one of those problems in moral philosophy which undergraduates are supposed to cut their teeth on,' Theodora said because in truth she could not bear the thought that a priest would be capable of murder. 'The answer could only be "If he were mad",' she concluded.

Lionel considered what he had learned of his boss over a ten-year period. Finally he said, 'I can imagine him killing someone in a temper, just lashing out. I don't know whether he's mad enough to plan any such act in advance.'

'What we need to do now, then,' Theodora said, 'is to divide the chase between us. We need to see the Wales, obviously.'

'I'll take Leslie. You take Kate.'

'She doesn't like me,' said Theodora.

'Well, I'm not that keen on Leslie. So we're quits. Then we need to see the Lees and Father Angel.'

'Yes, I agree about Angel,' Theodora said. 'Did we agree I'd do him?'

'He's the link between Cray and the diocese; if you like, between the Lees and the cathedral. And, actually, if you don't mind, I can do him tonight because I've been invited to be a governor of the primary school and he's the chair at this evening's meeting.'

Theodora loved the pride in Lionel's tone.

'Then we'll do the Lees together,' she said.

* * *

The number of deaf aids laid out on the table of St Sylvester's primary school hall at seven in the evening did not encourage Lionel. It reminded him of the Friends of the Cathedral who also had a high average age. He'd got to the school early in the hope of collaring Tobias Angel before the meeting and asking him about the land and the Lees and kindred matters.

'Father Toby won't be here till the last minute, seven fifteen,' said Orlando Groom. 'He doesn't care for idle chatter. Or, put it another way, the informal channels of communication bore him silly. Come and see the school.'

Lionel wondered where Orlando got his energy from, after a full day at the coalface, to be so bouncy and invigorated. Proudly Orlando showed him round half a dozen classrooms all crammed with displays of children's work, useful information about how to do elementary calculations and, since they were coming up to harvest festival, a plentiful display of the fruits of the earth. There were computers in every room and a portable video on a trolley in the main corridor. Lionel sought for the right thing to say.

'Display a great strength of the school?' he hazarded.

'Right,' said Orlando, clearly pleased. 'Ofsted said we weren't making the most of our display areas so we've rather gone to town to rectify the omission. I gave Mrs Trend, our key stage two coordinator, a scale point and hey presto.' He gestured to the overflowing walls.

'A Keatsian display,' Lionel tried. But this was a move too far for Orlando. The theme of harvest lay heavily in every classroom. Tins of baked beans marked the modern relation of the urban community to the seasons, but the natural world was not forgotten: apples lay in heaps, collages of autumn leaves were plentiful. In one victorious classroom there was a genuine sheaf of corn.

'Do these symbols of mortality give rise to any reflection on the part of the pupils?' Lionel asked. 'Do they feel the urge to sum up human life and wonder at its ephemeral quality?'

'No time,' said Orlando. 'They have the National Curriculum to get through. They leave that to the teachers.

We'd better get back to the hall; the governors will be filtering in.'

Lionel returned to the table full of deaf aids. He was introduced to a number of governors with the words, 'We're trying to recruit Mr Comfet to our body so we need to make a good impression.'

Lionel diverted himself by guessing which were Gainshurst and which Cray Martyr members. The vice chair, Mrs Court, was clearly Gainshurst. She shook Lionel warmly by the hand, enquired if he had coffee and an agenda, then delicately worked round to whether he had previous experience of being a governor or indeed of the work of schools in the maintained sector. She was enough of a diplomat to register no surprise when it emerged that although Lionel admitted to having taught in a prep school he hadn't stepped inside a state school before in his life.

'I keep thinking we need an induction course for our new members and you'd be exactly the man to try it out on, or indeed to get it together. You must stop us whenever you don't understand anything. We've got very jargonized with lots of initials over the last few years. Haven't we?' she shouted at the first deaf aid.

The aid turned a huge face towards her and frowned. 'We've a long way to go,' she said cryptically. Then she turned to the man on her right who was attempting both to fold his Zimmer frame and arrange his aid to make the best of the acoustics of the room. 'Yes?' she shouted.

'Long agenda tonight, Flo,' he obliged. Then he poked his other aided neighbour in the ribs and said, 'We lost every match, I see. So much for your famous coaching.'

The neighbour, smaller and fitter and with a degree of mobility denied to his colleague, swung his legs expertly round the table and collapsed the Zimmer. Its owner held on to the table and said, 'I said we lost every ma—'

'I heard you,' said the more able. 'The game's the thing, not the winning. Isn't that right, headmaster?'

'Teacher,' murmured Mrs Court. 'They have to be called headteachers nowadays.'

'Is that so?' said Lionel with interest. 'Why would that be?'

'Gender issues,' said Orlando breezily. 'Mustn't acknowledge sexual difference.'

'Dull old world that would be,' said the fat female deaf aid.

'Who's not coming?' Orlando was dispensing papers on the table and simultaneously offering a tray of powdered coffee. Lionel wondered how many jobs he could do at any one time. Perhaps this was just what primary school headteachers had to be good at. His eye turned to a coterie of tough-looking women talking hard over by the piano.

'Apologies from Mrs Tye,' said Lionel in a businesslike way.

'George Lawley will be late. He's got a date with a Chippendale chair, his words,' said Mrs Court.

Lionel was as cheered as any new boy at any school to know that he knew at least one governor, even a late one. He hadn't known that George was on the board. He would show him the ropes. Quid pro quo, Lionel thought, reflecting on all the times he had coached George over jumps.

'Parent governors,' Orlando whispered, indicating the piano knot. 'Feel they could run the school better than me. Will debate changing room facilities for hours on end but mention the curriculum and they fall asleep or leave the meeting.'

'Cray Martyr?' asked Lionel, testing out his theory.

'Just as bad as each other,' Orlando replied, catching his drift. 'But yes, that lot are.'

The church clock from St Sylvester's next door could be heard chiming the quarter and the door opened to admit the Reverend Tobias Angel.

'Good evening, chair. Dead on time.' Orlando had a coffee in his hand and a chair drawn for him before you could say knife.

Father Tobias swept the room with a fishy eye and lit on Lionel. 'Diocesan office come to spy on our humble affairs?'

'I understand you're a governor light,' said Lionel mildly. 'And since I'm due to retire in a month, I thought perhaps . . .'

Tobias relented. 'We shall need a skills inventory from you,' he said, but without malice.

'I've just been thinking about harvest.' Lionel waved to the various evidences of the concept round the room.

'An image of the Last Judgement,' said Father Tobias, in case Lionel should not know his Bible.

His words brought Lionel back to his real reason for being here at all. He edged a bit closer to Tobias and said, 'I wonder if I could have a word with you afterwards about the Lee business, just five minutes?'

Tobias nodded rapidly and banged with the end of a pencil on the table. 'Gentlemen, please, the hour has struck. In the name of the Father, the Son and the Holy Spirit.'

He prayed rapidly and the members of the governing body who were also members of his PCC made a good loud response.

'My intention is to end the meeting at nine o'clock wheresoever the business is at that hour. I'd like to change the order of agenda items two and five. And since I understand that Mrs Tye can't be with us I suggest we defer item four, boys' latrines, Mrs Tye's area of special interest, until the next meeting.'

He went at a tremendous rate. Lionel felt an immediate sense of relief. He attended so many bad meetings in the diocese that he'd almost forgotten what a good one could be like. He knew about agendaless meetings; lethargic and unfocused meetings; meetings which were held for no other purpose than to enhance the ego of the chair; meetings which were held because no one had the energy to cancel them; meetings rendered useless because half the members could not actually see the other half; meetings which were pointless because the business had already been fixed beforehand in the vestry, in the car park, by a phone call to the Bishop. Lionel was a connoisseur of bad meetings. The sign of a healthy institution lay in the quality of its meetings, in his view. The diocese suffered from the malaise of the Church in general. The primary school did not.

Tobias was excellent. He knew the business, he kept members to the point but encouraged everyone to contribute. It was an exercise in businesslike good manners. Lionel was much cheered. Local cooperative democracy for an unassailably good cause under the Church's common-sense leadership, he reckoned.

For twenty minutes Father Tobias steamed ahead at a steady cross-country canter through minutes of the last meeting ('You weren't here, Flo, so you can't object to them'); Local Education Authority business ('We can't stop them, so why debate it?' said the Zimmer and deaf aid man); amendments to school development plan ('Not enough time for sport,' said the unsuccessful coach. 'They'd need more than time,' said his antagonist).

Then they slowed down for the contentious bit. Tobias cleared his throat and said, 'Some of you will know that the developers have discovered the rural beauties of Cray Martyr. Hence item six, overspill expansion. The projection is three hundred new houses for first-time buyers within five years. That will have an effect on us.'

'I do feel our little school is just the right size for our kiddies at the moment. If we get any bigger the little ones will just get lost.'

Lionel thought, that's a Gainshurst response. He was right but also wrong. The Cray Martyr ladies had just the same reaction to incomers. The tones were more strident, the vowels more extreme but the same fear was present. 'They'll only look down on us' was the burden of the fear; 'we lived here first' the justification. Lionel wondered about the place of Mackenzie's All Foods superstore in all this. Here was certainly the reason why MAF would want to have a site and a road.

Father Tobias let the debate run and the fears release themselves. He won't encourage a conclusion or the taking up of positions which it might be later difficult to get out of, Lionel reckoned. And so it proved. The meeting was steered gradually to a close via a number of interesting items not of the first significance: school journey, PE curriculum policy, peripatetic music provision and the roof leak in the kitchen. 'I'd really rather it had leaked in a classroom,' Orlando complained. 'Teachers I can get, cooks never.'

As St Sylvester's clock struck nine, they were through. They exchanged the grace with vigour and began to disengage with the self-congratulatory feeling of work well done. Lionel sought out Orlando to thank him. He seemed surprised that anyone should pass a teacher a kind word.

'It's riveting,' Lionel assured him. 'I'd very much like to join you.'

'Spot on,' said Groom, heaving chairs back round the sides of the hall, collecting cups and sweeping papers into a plastic sack. 'I'll get the Archdeacon to propose you to the Board of Education.'

'Will they object?' Lionel thought of the old boot who ran the diocesan education department, a woman of advanced years not known for falling in with the wishes of others.

'They're desperate for members,' Groom reassured him. Outside, the remains of the autumn heat lingered in the darkness. Lionel caught Tobias Angel up as he made for the gap in the wicket fence with the sure tread of one who does it often.

'The Lees,' Lionel began.

'Whisky,' said Angel.

Together they stumbled down the lane between the school and the church and turned towards the back entrance of the vicarage. Sloping away below them was the valley at the farthest end of which was Giltchrist. Before them could be felt rather than seen the well-heeled suburbs of Gainshurst.

'Interesting cultural mix,' Lionel ventured.

'That's just what they don't do, mix. Particularly the Giltchrist crew. Your crew.'

Lionel thought he ought to get one or two things straight. 'As a layman I don't count as one of the Giltchrist crew. You know that. The senior cathedral clergy live in a world of their own quite untouched by reality. When they get up on their hind legs and tell governments how to govern and local authorities how to administrate they can do so totally untainted by knowledge or experience of any kind. They work a three-hour day; if their roof leaks they ring the diocesan office; they didn't have to apply for their jobs and it's no one's task to see they do anything.'

'And they're there for life.'

'Irremovable,' Lionel agreed.

'Spoilt rotten and unpleasant with it,' Angel said with relish.

'Meanwhile our communities,' Lionel nodded to Gainshurst and Cray Martyr, 'struggle on with too few resources of men and money. I mean religiously speaking.'

'No one goes into the Church for money. A secure social status for the feeble perhaps.'

Lionel wondered if he was thinking of his neighbour, Andrew Seamley.

'Of course, the two parishes, yours and Andrew Seamley's, are very different,' Lionel tested.

'Andrew's got his problems with some of his graves.' Angel grinned, but did not pursue the point. Abusing cathedral clergy might be all right in his book, but putting the boot into a fellow parish priest might not be. Lionel had met the distinction before. Angel turned into his back gate and steered Lionel across the uncut lawn to the back door of the vicarage.

The smell of fried fish mixed with incense hit them. The darkness was more intense inside the house. Angel showed no intention of switching on lights. Lionel stumbled along behind him, down a narrow passage, linoleum beneath his feet, until they reached a front ground-floor room. Then his host clicked the switch of a table lamp which originated a small pool of light in what looked like a study. There were books everywhere, on the table, on the floor, round three walls, in the chairs. Angel dislodged a couple of large volumes from the shelves behind the chimney piece, Cross's *Dictionary of the Church* and Kittel's *Biblia Hebraica*, and took out a bottle.

'Mrs Lee drinks it if I leave it about. But she hates books so it's safe behind there,' he explained.

The measure was generous. The taste reminded him of the smell of the house. Lionel realized he was drinking Laphroaig. The evening looked rosy.

'Just returning to your governors' meeting agenda,' Lionel resumed. 'The development of the area. Here would be a good place for a shopping mall?'

'So Sandy Mackenzie thinks.'

'Ah.' So Angel knew about MAF at least. Lionel began to explore his topic. 'Would he be able to get his articulateds in and out?'

'That would depend on whether the Lees would let him, wouldn't it?'

So he knew the score. Lionel peered through the gloom at his host. The large head with its beak-like nose and general air of the untamed stared back at him. On his own ground the priest's accent — Irish? Australian? — was more pronounced. The effect, Lionel realized, was to set him apart from the rest of the clergy, to suggest a classlessness, a freedom from the values and failings of the stereotypical 'vicar'.

'And Mick Lee's death?'

'Wasn't, I gather, an accident.'

Lionel wondered how much information to share with this rebarbative priest. 'I rang the police inspector before I came this evening,' he ventured. He waited. Angel said nothing, but gazed at him, smiling slightly.

'The wood which makes the scaffolding comes from a small subsidiary yard which used to belong to Elvestone's. The firm was taken over by—'

'Wale Holdings,' Angel completed.

'You're very well informed. Better than the cathedral chapter.'

'Not difficult,' Angel agreed.

'The systems for making sure that the scaffold boards are sound before they're put in place are, according to my man, quite tight. Everything is double-checked before it goes out of the yard.'

'Well, there you are then. Obviously any tampering must have been done at the cathedral site.'

'Why, in your opinion, should anyone want to tamper with scaffold boards to bring about Lee's death?'

Angel chewed his whisky. 'If the Lees have got a title to the access site, it would help a number of people if there was only one Lee brother to deal with rather than two if you wanted to do a deal.'

'And if there were no Lees at all?'

Angel considered. 'I expect there'd be a reverter on it. Most Church land is like that.'

'So it would come back to the Church.'

'It's a possibility.'

'Were all the Lee brothers aware of the possibilities of the land sale, would you know?'

'I've been in this parish fifteen years. You may revile the freehold but if they can't shift you it does mean that you have time to get to know your people. I'm baptizing the children of those I confirmed and married. They breed young, of course, round here. I've known all three Lee brothers since they were boys.'

'So did they all know of the land's possibilities?' Lionel pressed.

'I'll tell you which of the brothers did know about the land. It was the one your brother ran over, Jon.'

Lionel winced. 'It was an accident,' he said dully.

'That so?' Angel looked at him speculatively. 'I always thought he was the victim of a family feud.'

Lionel sat forward in his chair. 'What? What did you say? What feud?'

At that moment the door knocker sounded. Lionel jumped. It echoed through the house like the herald of death itself. Angel continued to look at his guest for a moment and then unfolded himself from his chair. 'Wait,' he said. 'If it isn't life and death, I'll get rid of them.'

But he didn't get rid. Instead there was the sound of a man's voice in the hall and a minute later Angel ushered George in.

George screwed up his eyes to adjust them to the peculiar mixture of light and gloom in the study. It took him a minute to recognize Lionel.

'Li, what are you up to? I just looked in to give my apologies for not getting to the governors' meeting. The chair proved a right beggar and once you start you can't stop for fear of the glue.'

'I was at the meeting as an apprentice,' Lionel returned. If they had to be interrupted by anyone at least George was the man he would have chosen.

Angel returned with another glass and they all sat down.

Lionel wasn't going to give up. 'Jon Lee was killed because of a family feud, not because my brother ran him over, you were saying.' He kept his voice level and expressionless.

Angel looked at George. 'You know the Lees, George. You wouldn't call them a pacific family, would you?'

'Nasty scrappers. Never fought fair and loved a fight, they did. Do.'

'What did you mean about a family feud?' Lionel pressed.

'The tale Jon Lee told me before he was killed was that your brother Vincent had approached him with an offer for the land behind the common. At the back here.' Angel gestured with his head. 'Vincent said that there might be as much as ten thousand in it if he, Jon, could prove a title to the land.'

'And could he?'

'Jon was sure his father, Mick Lee the elder, had the deeds but Mick Lee the elder was illiterate. Jon himself couldn't read either, and nor could his eldest brother Deke. The one who could was—'

'Mick Lee,' said George. 'The younger.'

'So what you're saying is that on the night Vincent was edging his way through the crowd outside the Plume of Feathers he was on his way to meet Jon Lee. To do what?'

'To see if the papers which Jon had dredged up were the title deeds and what they said about ownership.'

'How do you know?'

George looked across at Angel and grinned. 'I seem to remember you were there at the Plume that night, Father.'

'Well, I can read and I'm as silent as the grave,' said Angel from the half-darkness.

'And your theory is that one of the other brothers, Deke or Mick Lee the younger, thought that brother Jon was doing a deal behind their backs.'

There was a silence while Lionel thought this one over.

'You were both there that night?'

George nodded. 'Friday night is darts night.'

Angel said, 'I don't play darts but Jon had asked me to meet him there.'

'What exactly happened?' Lionel was on tenterhooks. If the story could get his brother released, even Mick Lee's death would not seem so important.

Angel said, 'Henry Lee, the little lad of Mick's, he was about seven at the time, came round here and said would I see his uncle in the Plume round eight o'clock. I went round about a quarter past. I've never worked out whether the Lees can tell the time but if they can they're always late. When I got there Jon wasn't there but old man Lee was. I sat down and waited and about half past Jon Lee came into the other half of the bar and looked round. His father had his back to him but Jon saw me and waved me to follow him outside. It was at that point that the fight broke out between the local lads and a contingent from the other end of the village. It wasn't particularly evil but the landlord pushed them all outside and then it got more serious. More joined in and I lost sight of Jon Lee. When I caught sight of him again, he was on the ground and there was someone belting hell out of him and tugging at his coat. I tried to reach him but I was tripped up. When I got up again, I saw Jon being run down the road towards your brother's car.'

Angel stopped.

'Then what?'

'I helped pull him off the car.'

'And then?'

'As I did so he said, "Mick's got it."'

'What did he mean?'

Angel shrugged. 'Jon Lee asked me there to read what he thought were the deeds to the land. I always assumed he was referring to that.'

'Why on earth didn't you tell the police?'

'Tell them what? There were no papers, deeds or anything else, on Jon's body. No one else came forward to say they'd seen Jon being run into your brother's car rather than your brother's car running into him.'

'But my brother is innocent. He never had any intention of killing anyone. He's stuck in that bloody awful prep school type place, looking after cucumbers, with the reputation of a drunken hit man. You should at least have tried . . .'

'Your brother was drunk, remember. And no one else came forward to back my statement.' Angel didn't even look uncomfortable. 'Life isn't meant to be fair. It's meant to be a classroom to prepare you for the next one. Maybe we need to be patient and watch the consequences work themselves out.'

'Where are the deeds now?'

It was George who enquired. He reckoned Lionel needed time to recover.

'If the Lees don't still have them, how about Wale?' Angel asked. 'He's involved in this somehow.'

Lionel sighed.

CHAPTER NINE: CHASING

The spaniel stood on his hind legs and hit the French windows with his front paws just below the catch. The door flew open and he departed for his breakfast at the Bishop's Palace. Theodora had no such luck. She drank Susan's coffee and nibbled Ryvita which tasted like lino.

'So I said you'd meet Kate at Andrew Seamley's parish centre round about eleven. That should give you plenty of time. I'll meet you for lunch and we can have a bite in Gainshurst.'

Theodora cheered up. A pub lunch in Gainshurst would be a lot better than the remains of last night's cheese salad at the Provost's Lodging.

'Are you sure that my meeting Kate is a good idea? I got the impression I wasn't her type of person.'

'Of course you're her type of person. You're both in orders. I realize she's further up the ladder than you but I expect you'll get there in the end. She's got a ten-year start on you.'

Theodora didn't know where to begin to refute this tissue of misrepresentation and thought it better not to try.

'Anyway, she sounded at the end of her tether when I rang. I think she's worried sick about Leslie. About whose accident, by the way, she's changed her tale. She now says he got mixed up in a pub brawl in Cray Martyr.'

Theodora thought this sounded familiar. 'Like Lionel's brother.'

'I thought he ran someone over.'

'Have the Wales told the police, I mean about Leslie's being beaten up?'

'I did ask. Kate said something about not wanting to cause any trouble.'

Theodora thought of what Lionel had told her of his conversation with Angel last night. Lionel had, against his custom, turned up to the cathedral's eight o'clock communion. Afterwards he and Theodora had paced round the lawns of the close and he had filled her in.

'Angel's line is that the Lees claim the title to the access land which MAF would need to make their superstore viable.'

'Claiming it isn't the same as proving it.'

'Exactly. And he also said,' Lionel had debated whether he would tell Theodora this, but he badly wanted to share his news with someone and he found her a sympathetic and discreet presence, 'Angel also said that on the night of Vincent's accident he was at the Plume of Feathers and he saw someone running Jon Lee towards Vincent's car.'

Theodora had grasped his point immediately. 'Someone ran Jon on to Vincent's car rather than Vincent running his car into Jon?'

'Right.'

'Who?'

'He didn't know. I inferred that he thought it was Deke.'

'Why didn't Angel say so at the time?'

'No witnesses, he said. And also,' Lionel had hesitated, 'I got the impression that Angel was on the Lees' side, that he wanted them to win.'

'What sort of win?'

'It was almost as though he felt they had the right to any goody which could come from their having the land title.'

'Well, that's surely correct.'

'If it had been Mick Lee, I'd have agreed, but Deke Lee is just a thug.'

'You can't have a world in which legal entitlement depends on niceness of character,' Theodora had objected reasonably.

'How about we see the Lees this morning?' Lionel had said. 'If I pick you up at ten we could brave them together. And before that I'm going to do a bit of research via my old City contacts into the affairs of Wale Holdings.'

Lionel had paced on to the diocesan office. Theodora had returned to what passed for breakfast at the Provost's Lodging.

'So I'll drop you off at the St Andrew's centre at eleven and pick you up at twelve and you can tell me everything Kate says.' Susan was running on.

Theodora wondered if Susan had heard of confidentiality, or even discretion.

'I'm going with Lionel to see the Lees first,' Theodora interposed.

'They won't take you long. Get Lionel to drop you at St Andrew's then I'll pick you up from there. You've got to see Kate. I promised you would. And keep your eye on the ball,' Susan admonished. 'I want to know if Kate and Leslie Wale's troubles are connected with Reggie's and Mick Lee's.'

'Well, why don't you interview Kate yourself then?'

'Oh, you're so much more experienced at that sort of thing than me,' Susan said winningly.

* * *

'It's a different world,' Lionel said as he pulled into the lay-by opposite the Lees' fields.

Ragwort grew in greater strength than grass which had been over-grazed for many seasons. There was a veritable plumber's shop at one end of the field beside the caravan. Old taps and basins and yards of wire were tangled together. There was a litter of beer cans stacked in an empty and wheelless pram. As Lionel and Theodora made their way across the worn grass a black lurcher bitch, tied up with a clothes line, edged her way out from under the van and began to bark, wagging her tail and flattening her ears at the same time.

'I can think of no circumstances in which we should be welcome here,' Theodora said, 'let alone the present ones.'

'I did manage a word with Mrs Lee the other day when she collected the children from school.'

'Make any headway?'

'Not as such.'

As they spoke a small boy, solid and dark-haired, emerged from the van backwards carrying a bundle of tools.

'Hello, Henry,' said Lionel.

'Grandma's not in,' said the boy, not exactly addressing them but throwing the words in their direction.

'When will she come back?'

The boy didn't answer. Instead he went to where the lurcher bitch had sat down at the end of her tether and joined her on the ground.

'Has she gone far?' Theodora enquired. She liked all dogs and let the lurcher smell her hands and feet, then squatted to fondle her under the ear. The lurcher rolled over on her back and invited further and more intimate attentions. Theodora obliged.

'She's gone down Cray for the shops.' The boy appeared to be mollified by his dog's acceptance of Theodora. 'She won't be back soon,' he added to discourage any optimism on the part of his visitors. As he spoke he began to unwrap the bundle and take out the tools one by one. He didn't exactly clean them but scanned them, brushed them with a bit of old towelling and laid them separately on the ground. There were two sorts of jemmy, a lever, a chisel and cold hammer and some wooden wedges.

'Building something?' Lionel enquired.

'Nope,' said Henry. Then, as the dog continued to bang her tail against the ground at Theodora's attentions, and the feeling of their being a group began to develop, he added, 'Hunting.'

'What do you hunt?' Lionel pursued. His tone, though, was interested without being intrusive.

'Got to find the papers.'

Lionel surveyed the mixture of tools. 'Hidden deep, are they?'

'Difficult to say,' said Henry, perhaps imitating someone else's tone. 'Some of them are very deep, some of them just under the sod.'

Theodora thought, it's like one of those party games I was no good at as a child. One player describes some object of which another then guesses the identity. Lionel, however, she noticed, seemed to be pursuing some orderly line of inquiry. Perhaps he already had a theory. 'Is it best to try and take them at night?' he asked.

'Oh, yes,' Henry agreed. 'Can't catch papers daytime.' He seemed to regard Lionel as a fellow hunter.

'Have you tried up St Sylvester's way yet?'

A look of cunning took its place on Henry's concentrated features. 'Nah, not Sylvester's,' he said contemptuously. 'Andrew's, up Gainshurst.'

'Had any luck?' Lionel asked. He might have been enquiring about a fishing catch.

'Early days,' said Henry.

'Or nights,' Lionel offered.

Henry enjoyed the joke hugely.

* * *

The mist which had lain in the valley between Cray Martyr and Giltchrist earlier in the morning was beginning to dissolve as Theodora and Lionel walked away from Henry Lee. The edge of the field had a scattering of litter blown up against the diverse types of material which marked the boundary of the Lees' domain. Old plastic wrappings were deeply woven into the desiccated roots of the hawthorn hedge; pieces of wooden clothes horse and a bit of a TV cabinet lent their support to the tangled wire which took over when the bushes gave out.

'I'm never too sure whether their total disregard for aesthetics or indeed for efficiency is a sign of sturdy independence and creative originality or just feckless idleness,' Lionel remarked.

'Perhaps it's to mark themselves off from the excessive neatness of suburbia. I'm not sure *I* could live in Gainshurst.'

'Ought we to hang about and see if we can make contact with some of the other Lees?' Lionel enquired, scanning the bleak, disfigured plot of ground.

'We keep saying we ought to see the Lees and not doing it,' Theodora agreed. 'I suppose we're frightened of them.'

'They *are* alien. I find it difficult to read any of them. Even poor Mick, whom I saw every day and whose courage I did very much admire, I wouldn't say I had a relationship with. And Henry's headteacher has a similar difficulty with his pupil.'

'They always sound to me as though English isn't their first language, and yet I doubt whether many of these travellers who gave up travelling a couple of generations ago have any other tongue.'

'They always make me feel as though I'm the intruder, as though they were here first and the land is theirs,' Lionel said.

'I suspect we feel guilt at many levels about travellers and that makes us behave badly towards them and they reciprocate.'

'And by all accounts the eldest brother, Deke, is a shocker.'

'Of course, the person who isn't frightened or guilty about the Lees is—'

'Tobias Angel,' Lionel finished for her.

'Why would you say that was?'

'A genuinely religious man.'

'In the sense that?'

'He doesn't care a toss about worldly or personal advancement or the opinions of society. He doesn't want to gain anything for himself and he's prepared to leave to Providence much that the rest of us think we could arrange better ourselves.'

'You mean that, in a sense, Angel is on the edge of society in the same way as the travellers.'

'It's not the way the Church of England's clergy are generally perceived,' Lionel assented, 'but, yes, that's true. He stands aloof and judges us.' He glanced at Theodora. 'You seem to have got his measure. Perhaps it takes one to know one.'

'Oh, I'm not in his class.' Theodora thought of her unfinished biography of Thomas Henry Newcome. 'I'm not without ambition. It's just that I tend to exempt myself on the grounds that scholarly research doesn't count as the worst sort: it has connections with truth.'

'So Angel supported the Lees in the bypass row because they're underdogs and he's just doing the same again in the MAF deal.'

'That's my guess,' Theodora agreed.

They had turned towards the gate and the road as though they had tacitly made the decision to abandon their task. But as they reached the gate there came the sharp eager clatter of hooves on the tarmac of the lane. Tobias Angel appeared, hanging on to the end of the head collar rope of his Connemara.

'Could you open the gate?' Angel asked, gesturing to the opening in the hedge of the field opposite their own. 'Normally he's perfectly manageable but he's just seen that smart new Arab mare from your Equestrian Centre and he thinks he'd like to improve the acquaintance.'

Together Lionel and Theodora lifted the cumbersome gate from its bed of mud and swung it open enough to admit Christopher who sprang forward, bucking and snorting to show what a fine fellow he was.

Angel leaned on the gate and gazed after his pony. 'Sex makes fools of us all,' said the celibate priest with pride.

'We came up to see the Lees,' Lionel volunteered. 'But in the end the only one available was young Henry.'

'Best of the bunch,' Father Tobias agreed. 'Much the cleverest and no violence in him — yet.'

'We gained the impression that it was he who had been taking a hammer to Mr Seamley's tombs up at St Andrew's,' Theodora offered.

Father Tobias showed no surprise. 'Did he say why?'

Theodora glanced at Lionel to see how much he wanted to reveal of their inquiries.

'I think he may have heard his elders discussing the title deeds to the land. This bit.' Lionel waved his hand at the Lees' field. 'Perhaps they spoke of them as hidden or buried and Henry made his own connections. Some of his family are buried in the graveyard of St Andrew's, after all.'

Angel ceased to lean on his gate and gazed across the road at the Lees' land. 'I'd hate MAF to get its hands on this bit of paradise,' he said.

'Would the Lees sell?' Lionel asked.

'They regard small bits of land much as they once regarded their vans, as sacred spaces, not to be violated. It's theirs. Where else would they keep their horses and pursue their trades, such as they are?'

'Where are the deeds, do you know?' Theodora enquired.

'The night Vincent ran down Jon Lee, I thought they might have found their way into Deke's pocket. But there's no proof of that. And if Deke is talking about them being hidden or lost, it suggests that someone else might have got their hands on them, or they may have just disappeared in the mêlée.'

'Who does own the land, in your opinion?' Theodora was direct.

Angel turned his eagle countenance towards her and smiled. 'Without the deeds, who can say?'

'And where would they be kept officially, I mean besides in the possession of the Lees?'

'Ah, Miss Braithwaite, I'm sure I need not point out the possible sources to an historian who has been published in the *Church History Review*.'

Theodora was surprised. She felt she'd done nothing to warrant the attack. Angel had a true religious sense, but he also had shortcomings. He definitely didn't care for women, or — Theodora was ever honest with herself — perhaps it was just her.

'Meanwhile young Henry does his bit for the family by digging up the graveyard at Gainshurst,' Lionel said to restore harmony.

'A good lad,' Angel approved.

* * *

The Reverend Andrew Seamley was very proud of the architect-designed adaptation of his north transept into a parish centre. Any criticism on the part of his fellow clergy of his use of holy ground for selling coffee he put down to envy. And in a way, Theodora tried as ever to be fair, he's right. It's no bad thing for parishioners to have a meeting space and somewhere to fraternize. It's just somehow there are plenty of such spaces but very few of the other sort, the sort dedicated to worship. It set up the wrong resonances, too; the Formica and carpet covering more ancient materials created a dissonance. Fluorescent strip lights swung only just out of the way of customers' heads. Plastic chairs wobbled on the uneven floor. But four hundred years of prayer was not so easily banished. The atmosphere lingered oppressively on and customers tended to sip their coffee quietly and converse in lowered tones. Theodora looked round. The room was empty apart from a man at the far end playing draughts with himself.

As in all such places run by volunteers it took time to get anything going. First one had to attract the attention of the coven of dedicated conversationalists secreted behind the kitchen door. Theodora cleared her throat a couple of times but nothing happened. She considered hurling the ashtrays through the window and taking all her clothes off, but decorum prevailed. When at last one lady of advanced years swung her replaced hips spryly towards the counter to refresh her own cup, she appeared overcome with astonishment at the sight of Theodora.

'I didn't know there was anyone *waiting*,' she said with resentment. 'Would you like something?'

'Coffee?'

'Coffee?' queried the old one as though this was an outlandish request.

'Would be very nice,' Theodora lied.

It took time to find the coffee urn, top it up with hot water, return to the back parlour for the best advice about where to locate the cups, unearth them and unite coffee, water and crockery in one tremendous feat of coordination.

'I'm expecting a friend.' Theodora thought it only fair to warn the elderly one, just in case she should want to get a flying start on the preparations.

'Sufficient unto the day,' responded the other wisely and with remarkable speed returned to the salon out back.

Kate was late and when she did arrive Theodora had plenty of time to observe her entry. It happened at a moment when the old one had made a brief appearance in search of digestive biscuits. Kate flung open the door and paused on the threshold. The elder looked up and offered effusive greeting.

'Kate dear, how lovely, it's ages. You don't look at all well.'

How could she tell beneath the formidable make-up Kate was wearing, Theodora wondered. Kate was gorgeously arrayed, richly dight, Theodora thought to herself. She wore a greenish-bluish woollen dress and a crimson armless jacket which looked vaguely Indian. She clanked from every limb: gold bangles, a girdle of amber round her waist, a rope of jet round her neck and dangling jet earrings. Once free of the attentions of the old coffee server, she swept across the room to Theodora and embraced her on each cheek.

She began with the usual protestations of being overworked, up to her eyes, pressed for time, only able to spare a moment. Theodora, who had moved among clergy all her life in her father's parish, in her own education and training as a curate, found time to wonder during this recital why only senior clergy indulged in this sort of fantasy. Parish priests, many of whom were responsible for three or four churches, complained rather less. Certainly the cathedral clergy had little enough to do, being required to attend three services a day in the cathedral one month in every four. She let Kate talk herself out. When the coffee came, Kate grew calmer and less frenetic. Finally, she said, 'Susan tells me you're a sleuth.'

Theodora reckoned she wasn't going to get anywhere by being self-deprecating and that, given a bit of help, this scatty, silly woman might well have enough local knowledge to be useful. 'Yes,' she said. 'And you have need of one, I gather.'

For a moment it looked as though Kate was going to go back to overdrive. Then suddenly she seemed to subside. Physically she slumped, and the line where the facial make-up finished and met the un-made-up neck made her look as though she were wearing a mask which had been dislodged.

'It's Leslie and the Lee thing,' she said. 'You saw what happened on Saturday night. Well, I said I thought he'd had an accident on one of his sites. Wale Holdings has about half a dozen going at any one time. Leslie's been terribly, terribly successful. You know he started from nothing and just worked and worked.'

Theodora realized that this was going to be the pattern of Kate's recounting. A nugget of useful truth would be sandwiched in between a lot of boasting and inflation. Theodora would only need to prompt and sift. She was expert; she knew her strength.

'Well, of course, success like Leslie's attracts envy,' Kate hurried on. 'Local boy makes good and all that. He knows a lot of people in Cray Martyr who resent what he's done for them.'

'What has he done for them?'

'He's a developer. He develops. He cares passionately about people,' Kate wailed. 'He's done so much to help get the new bypass.'

'I didn't know there was going to be one.'

'It's been on hold for years. But it will come, Leslie says, and when it does it will really revitalize the area. And, I don't know if you know this, but MAF have got their eye on a site round the back of the church and Leslie will be acting for them.'

'All controversial stuff.'

'It oughtn't to be. It's all for the good of the community.'

'The Lees?' Theodora prompted.

'I knew them,' Kate admitted. 'We both knew them. I mean the brothers. I knew them all when we were young. Before we started out. Mick was the nicest. Jon was just a boy. Deke, the eldest, was the nastiest. He's grim. They used to call him a nutter.'

Theodora was interested to see the vocabulary of the canon had reverted to her pre-Christian youth. 'Leslie's accident on Saturday night?' she prompted again.

'It wasn't an accident. He got a call to say would he go to the Plume of Feathers. One of Mack's men wanted to see him.'

'The Mackenzie of MAF?'

'Right. Well, naturally he went and waited a bit. There was no one there from Mack's. So he started to leave but as he was getting into the Jag three men grabbed him and . . .' Kate couldn't bring herself to go on.

'Reduced him to the state we saw him in.'

'Yes.'

'Who and why?'

'Leslie says one of them was Deke Lee.'

'Because?'

'Leslie thinks that Deke thinks Leslie was responsible for Mick Lee's death.'

'How responsible?'

'Deke thinks Leslie contrived faulty scaffold boards.'

'You mean actually took a saw and rendered some of them unsafe?'

Kate nodded.

'Why should Deke think that Leslie wanted Mick Lee dead?'

'Deke thinks that Leslie is out to kill off the Lees so that the land comes back to the Church. The Church would sell but the Lees wouldn't.'

Theodora digested this. 'Is that likely or possible?'

'Of course not.'

'But it would have to be someone who knew the movements of the scaffolders and the precise tasks of each of them. That would only be known by the site manager. And the site manager takes his instructions from Leslie?'

'He's one of Leslie's employees, yes.'

'Let's get this clear. Are the Lees, or anyway Deke, saying that Leslie or the site manager tampered with the boards?'

'Leslie thinks that Deke Lee thinks Leslie knew from the site manager who did what on the cathedral site and that Leslie made the boards unsafe.'

'When were the boards put in place?'

'Leslie says he told the police all he knew about the boards and that the site manager confirmed what he said. The new lot of boards were delivered on Thursday evening just as the men were going home. They weren't needed until Friday afternoon. They were put in place round about three o'clock on Friday.'

'Whose job would it have been to put them in place?'

'Leslie says each man put up his own boards when he needed them.'

'So Mick Lee put them in place himself?'

'That's what the site manager says.'

Theodora shuddered. 'So Mick Lee contrived his own death.'

'Yes. It must have been an accident.' Kate thought about this and had another go. 'Or rather if the boards were tampered with he was responsible for not checking them.'

'But Mick Lee's brother doesn't think that.'

'No,' Kate agreed.

'And someone did tamper with the boards, after all.'

'Yes, I suppose so. I mean the police are saying that.'

'And could that have been Leslie?'

'No, of course not. I told you. Leslie was nowhere near the site on Friday.'

'Would he be able to prove that?'

'His office will vouch for him. His girl, Stephanie, is very reliable.'

'Why didn't Deke Lee go to the police if he thought your husband was responsible for his brother's death?'

Kate seemed to think this was an odd idea. 'The Lees aren't like that,' she said. 'They're travellers. Only they haven't really travelled for years. Their grandfather was the last to be on the road. But that's their culture all the same. They wouldn't dream of mixing with the police. They decide what has to be done and do it themselves. They don't use other people's systems.'

'If Deke Lee did beat up your husband, why don't you go to the police?' Theodora nearly added, you're not a traveller.

'You don't understand. The Lees are dangerous. I think Deke got someone to have a go at me earlier on Saturday.' Kate told Theodora about the car outside the off-licence in Gainshurst high street.

'And you didn't report that to the police?'

'Leslie and I talked it over. We thought best not.'

'So what do you intend to do now?' Theodora didn't see why she should spare Kate.

'I hoped, I wondered, I mean Susan Tye said, couldn't you find out who the real killer was? If it wasn't Leslie, someone must have been responsible for the boards being faulty.'

Theodora considered. 'The way in to a killing is to ask why anyone should want to do it. Who would want Mick Lee dead?'

'How on earth should I know?' Kate seemed to think she had done her bit and it was up to Theodora now. Indeed, Theodora reflected, she'd been a mine of information. The only problem was how much did Theodora believe. She felt an urgent need to talk to Lionel.

'Can you just go over the reasons why Deke Lee thinks it was Leslie who wanted Mick dead?'

Kate showed signs of tearfulness. Really, Theodora thought, they don't breed canons like they used to. If the Church is going to put women in high places they need to pick a good deal more carefully than they have so far.

* * *

The Docklands headquarters of Wale Holdings was a building site. JCBs, cement mixers, and piles of that essential stuff of any modern construction, breeze blocks, made access difficult. Building largely consists of reversing lorries and there were a lot of these about. The actual office rose above its foundation of machines and piles, thrusting upwards to fourteen completed storeys.

Callers were not allowed to park on the forecourt because the tarmac had not yet set and the last two cars which had done so had sunk up to their hubcaps. Lionel, chatting in his affable way with the doorman, ascertained that there had been trouble letting the units even though they had a splendid view over the remains of the mud chute and across the Thames to Blackwall. In fact, the doorman confided, Wale Holdings was the sole occupant at the moment. They thought they'd made a letting last week to MI6 but it turned out to be a false alarm.

Lionel had secreted his ancient car in a cul-de-sac created by a front-line defence of concrete mixers drawn up like tanks and a crane with two flat tyres which, Lionel reckoned, wasn't going to be moved in a hurry. It wasn't so unlike certain sorts of battlefield he had known. He liked these small logistical calculations which had formed part of his military youth.

Once inside the building things became a lot more efficient, or anyway tightly controlled. The friendly doorman was replaced by a decorative eighteen-year-old girl whose job description was geared to keeping people out or shaping them into Wale Holdings-sized nuggets. She delved deep into Lionel's past and present status and future intentions before issuing him with a 'Visitor to Chairman' sticky label which she urged him to attach to his person and on no account to be parted from.

'Or I'll end up in room 101,' Lionel joked, but the allusion was lost on the beauty.

'Security have their orders,' she said austerely and bade him sit down.

Twenty minutes passed. No one entered or left. At infrequent intervals the girl turned the pages of something which she kept below the level of the counter. Lionel had exhausted the wonders of the *Architectural Review* and the *Cement Industry* before a buzzer broke the heavy silence of the insulated waiting room.

'Mr Wale is at his desk now, if you'd care to go through.'

Lionel, to whom the phrase was new, imagined that for the last twenty minutes Leslie had been in yogic practice on the floor and was now able to get up and stagger to the more usual location. He went through or rather up fourteen floors in a lift one side of which was made of glass so that he could enjoy the view over the river. Lionel, who was not good at heights, crouched on the far side of the box and reached his destination with relief.

Leslie Wale's office had the same unfinished air as the Tyes' house. Lionel had expected state-of-the-art modernity with banks of computers showing graphics of Wale Holdings' prospering enterprises. Instead the main items in the room were a rowing machine and a large round table with a glass top and two downmarket canvas chairs. Behind the table and indeed gripping its edge sat Leslie Wale. The day was warm, and two sides of the room were glass, but even so it seemed to Lionel that Leslie was sweating more than a healthy man should. Leslie had a striped blue and white shirt, a red tie, which was not in touch with his collar, and no jacket.

Other men's nervousness always made Lionel preternaturally relaxed. It was no virtue on his part; he did exactly the same with nervous horses. It was an instinct unrelated to courage, but it had made him a dependable soldier. Now he smiled confidently at Leslie.

'Mr Wale, how very good of you to see me. We did meet I think many moons ago when you used to do business with my brother, Vincent Comfet.'

This opening gambit did not seem to diminish Leslie's nervousness. He made a sort of attempt to rise but achieved only the movement of a man who might like to be sick.

'Lionel, of course, couldn't quite place you for a minute. Sit down. How about some . . .' he paused as though there might be some question about what one would drink at four in the afternoon, 'tea?'

'Lovely,' said Lionel, drawing up his canvas chair and placing it exactly opposite Leslie's own at the glass table, sitting down very squarely and placing his document case with obvious precision beside him.

Leslie continued to stare at Lionel as though he hadn't heard him, as if, indeed, he was listening for some remoter sound. Then he got up as though it pained him and made for the window sill and pressed an internal phone.

'Steph? Two teas now, dearie, there's a good girl.'

Lionel wondered if Leslie kept dogs. Leslie continued to look out of the window in an abstracted way and then limped back to the table. Lionel smiled kindly at him while he settled. Then he began. 'A couple of rather tricky matters I need your help with.' His tone was confiding. 'You may know I work for the diocesan set-up at Giltchrist Cathedral.'

Leslie nodded and muttered, 'Seem to remember Vince mentioning it.'

'Of course, previously the builders concerned with the cathedral's restoration work were Elvestone's. That's right, isn't it?'

'I believe so.'

'But you must be certain. You took them over,' Lionel edged his papers from his document case and consulted his list, 'with a two-thirds majority on the board. Yes?'

'Yes.'

'How much supervision do you exercise over the actual building works?'

'What? How do you mean supervision?'

'Wale Holdings has three building companies, two machine leasing companies and a small paint manufacturing plant outside Huddersfield. I just wondered how much direct management you were able to exercise with that span of interest.'

'You seem to know a lot about us.' Leslie's tone aimed at the belligerent but it quavered. What was the man frightened of?

'Yes. I've done my prep.' Lionel was complacent. 'But, as I said, I've got two little problems on my hands. One of your workmen, Mick Lee, was killed while repairing our cathedral. We shall need to be sorting out your insurance to see it's as generous as possible to the family.'

Leslie Wale said, 'Kate's mentioned it. It'll all be dealt with by our insurers. No need to worry about that.'

'My worry is different,' said Lionel. 'What I need to know, and indeed my committee will need to know, is how are you able to embark on this restoration project without any financial guarantees from the diocese.'

There was a long silence. Lionel went on. 'As far as I can see from my perusal of the available documentation, and I'm surprised to find how little of that there is, you are funding the diocese to the level of about fifty thousand a quarter.' He leaned a little nearer to Leslie. 'How are you able to do that? And, indeed, why should you do it?'

Leslie gazed down through the glass table at his shoes. When at last he raised his head to look at Lionel, Lionel thought he was going to collapse, he looked so ill. He was saved from summoning help by the entrance of Stephanie, bearing tea. There was a moment's disengagement while the tray was managed and the girl withdrew. Then Leslie said, as though Lionel had not asked his question, 'We've come a long way, you know, Kate and me. We've both gone up in the world, climbed every mountain like.'

Lionel nodded, content to give the man time to recover himself.

'This is the fourteenth storey,' Leslie said as though this must be impressive. 'I always reckoned on and up and the fourteenth storey is pretty well up, don't you think?'

'If you measure success in storeys, I suppose it must be,' was all Lionel could think of.

'And the glass lifts, they're a feature. You know.'

Because he could think of nothing much to say to this Lionel said, 'Difficult to let though, office space I mean, at present.'

It was a bad choice. Leslie banged his hand on the glass table-top and began to talk frenetically. He got up and went back to the window sill and rolled a cardboard map cylinder from a pile of such things.

'Look,' he said, 'look at the whole project.' He had difficulty shaking the paper from its tubular container but resisted Lionel's attempts to help. Finally he got it rolled out on the table, its springy ends held down by a cup of tea and a mobile phone.

'Look, you can change the face of the land and change how people live. You can give them better, smarter, more convenient ways of living.'

Lionel saw that what was being shown him was a map of the Gainshurst-Cray Martyr borders. Lionel could see the school and the church.

'It's just a matter of getting the infrastructure right, getting roads through and getting people to understand about the housing. Traffic flow, pedestrian flow balance.' Leslie was gabbling. 'You can be really creative, you know, like God. You can design whole ways of life, how people relate, how they can be neighbours like it used to be.'

Lionel had a fleeting vision of the terraces in old Cray Martyr which the new bypass had been going to destroy. Had Leslie really seen the scheme in those terms? He had a sudden intuition of what Leslie was about and what he was going to say next.

'But there's always someone in the way,' Leslie plunged on. 'There's always some bit of land you can't get at or some bastard who holds the whole thing up. They simply don't share the vision. Isn't it awful how "progress" has become a no-no? A dirty word you can't use in polite company?'

He turned to look at Lionel and for the first time in their meeting offered him eye contact. 'I play golf at the Royal Gainshurst and there was a bloke in the clubhouse last week saying we don't want any more changes round here for another couple of centuries. We ought to just stop building buildings and roads and live off what we've got. What we've got, for Christ's sake. Can't he see what we've got is just a set of seedy dysfunctional slums for seedy dysfunctional people? They all need changing . . . I mean is he bloody mad or am I?'

'But you can't change people's characters by building roads and putting them into housing units they don't want to go into and which are actually rather hard to make user-friendly. Any change in human life has to be freely embraced and worked for. Nothing else seems to work.' Lionel was surprised to find himself talking back to this unhappy man as though he was sane, when clearly he wasn't.

'There's always someone in the way,' Leslie repeated as though it were a mantra.

'You mean the Lees got in your way,' Lionel said gently.

Leslie seemed surprised. 'Lees?' he said. 'No, I can deal with the Lees. No, it's your lot.'

'Our lot?'

'The cathedral.'

'I don't follow.'

It looked for a moment as though Leslie would draw back. But then the pressure of his emotion and the strain of the last twenty-four hours seemed to get the better of him.

'Your lot, the Provost and Chapter. They own so much land round Cray Martyr whichever way you turn you've got to deal with them. I thought that was what you'd come about.' Leslie turned a bleary eye towards Lionel. 'Isn't it?'

'Leslie,' said Lionel, moving round the table to get a more comforting line on him, 'why don't you tell me all about it and we'll see what we can do to help you.'

CHAPTER TEN: WINNING

'Is Theodora there?'

'Is that you?'

'Susan?'

'Lionel?'

'Yes. Could I have a quick word with Theodora?'

'Are you getting anywhere?'

'How do you mean?'

'Have you seen Leslie Wale?'

'Yes. I ran him to earth this afternoon.'

'And?'

'In the end he was really quite helpful. Perhaps more than he knew.'

'Do you know who killed Lee and is Reggie the victim of blackmail?'

'It's just possible we can make a step or two forward. If I could just talk to Theodora?'

'I know she's the sleuth and I'm not.' Susan was without irony. 'But it is *my husband* who's in distress.'

'Yes, I know. I do see your point but we need to, Theo and I, need to just get one or two things straight and it would be easier if . . .'

'I quite understand. I'll get Theo to ring you the moment she gets back. She's just walking Jasper at the moment.'

'Who?'

'The dog.'

'Oh, right. In that case could you say I'll be at the Plume of Feathers in Cray Martyr between seven and eight?'

'Rightie ho.'

* * *

The Plume of Feathers at seven thirty was almost empty. Its two bars, in 1900s mahogany with engraved mirrors behind them, shone with reflected light. Theodora, who liked pubs she did not know — you never knew what you might find in them — sipped shandy happily and reviewed the faded sepia photographs of jolly Eastenders picking hops in long-abandoned hop fields.

She reviewed what she had learned from Kate Wale. What it came down to in essence was that Leslie *did* have a reason to kill Mick Lee. He didn't want anyone contesting the purchase of the land for the hypermarket. Moreover, Leslie had the opportunity to tamper with the scaffold planks since he'd known about the routine for putting them in place and might easily have gone down on Thursday night to cut them. If Kate was right, the surviving Lee brother, Deke, also reckoned it was Leslie who had killed his brother and hence was bent on revenge. It remained to be seen what Lionel had got out of his Wale.

Lionel put down a pint of Flowers keg bitter and settled himself opposite Theodora.

'The heart of the matter is Reggie and Marcus More.' Lionel sounded complacent.

'You sound glad,' Theodora remarked.

'I always thought More wasn't just inept and unpleasant. All that pseudo-scholarly stuff hid a criminal nature.'

'Reggie's not a criminal, is he?' She thought of Susan.

'Just your average frightened clerical bungler.'

'So fill me in.'

'Wale said,' Lionel began, 'MAF gave him a brief to find out who owned the land for the access way. Wale set Vincent on the matter as Vincent told us. Vincent contacted the Lees and developed a working relationship with Jon Lee, the youngest brother.'

'Then the accident put the lid on that,' Theodora surmised.

'Right. When Vince was out of the game, Wale himself took over. Things went quiet for a bit then about three months ago—'

'Round about June this year?' Theodora enquired.

'Yes. Wale began to be pressed by MAF. So he contacted the diocese.'

'Why didn't he go through Kate?'

'He didn't want too many people to know, and anyway he doesn't confide his business to Kate. I don't know whether he thinks she might disapprove of the shadier bits or not.'

'So who did he get?'

'He got Veronica Lure.'

'Hardly a person of influence. Would she have known?'

'Mrs Lure is secretary to both Reggie and Marcus. She likes to think, firstly, that she knows everything, and secondly that it's unkind to disappoint anyone.'

'And what did Mrs Lure tell Leslie?'

'She told him that the land was owned by the Lees.'

'Which is correct.'

'Well, that's rather the crux. Apparently, she later rang back and said she'd been wrong. Almost unheard of, I must admit, for Mrs L to frame those words.'

'So who did own the land, then?'

'Wale's story is that Mrs L said she'd checked and the Church owned the land.'

'What had made her change her mind?'

'That's just the point. Wale says Mrs L had checked with Marcus More and he'd looked at the file and been through the documents and there was clear evidence that the access road land was part of a bigger lot which the Church had always owned. Any suggestion that the Lees owned it was a mistake. They had a lease on a bit of it which had come to the end with the death of the grandfather in 1974. After that it was clear that the land reverted to the original owner, the Church.'

'But the Church had done nothing about the land since then.'

'Right.'

'Unbelievable.'

'On the contrary. You'd hardly believe the number of charitable trusts, even of land, the Church either doesn't know it has or, if it does, administers quite waywardly without any reference to the conditions of the original grant.'

'They only start looking if there's a lot of money at stake, like here.'

'Exactly.'

'So what else?'

'After he'd had his conversation with Mrs Lure, Leslie got hold of Marcus More and asked to see the documents and have the lawyers check them.'

'Sensible.'

'Only More then said he couldn't produce them.'

'Why?'

'He prevaricated as only Marcus can. First he said they were confidential.'

'Isn't that absolutely Church,' Theodora exclaimed. 'What on earth did he expect Leslie to do? Give him the purchase price on his say-so?'

'Something like that.'

'Then?'

'Then he said they weren't currently available.'

'Meaning?'

Lionel stopped and nibbled a free nut. 'That they were lodged in some other place.'

'Such as?'

'Kew,' said Lionel, who was enjoying himself.

'Kew equals the Land Registry.' Theodora's research skills were all in place.

'Or Lambeth Palace, or St Sylvester's Betterhouse.'

'The original trustees,' Theodora surmised.

'Right.'

'So why hadn't Marcus More got hold of them to show them to Leslie?'

'Precisely. And by this time, of course, MAF, months down the road from their original inquiries, dates for planning permission applications heaving into view, were getting shirty with Wale.'

'So what did they do?'

'Sir Sandy rang up his livery company's chaplain.'

'Reggie.'

'The very same.'

'And?'

'This is the bit Wale is not sure about. He, Wale, acting on Sir Sandy's directions, came and saw Reggie in the office and what Wale remembers him as saying was that he could get the title deeds for MAF but it would cost.'

'The million for the restoration fund,' Theodora said.

Lionel grinned and nodded. 'Reggie the entrepreneur.'

'Difficult to believe.'

'And so it proved. Reggie says More can't let the originals out of his custody but has produced a set of copies.'

'Copies are no good,' said Theodora. 'Why can't Reggie or Marcus let Wale or MAF see the originals?'

'That is the point.'

'Let's suppose the originals say the title to the land is the Church's and the sale would bring a million pounds to the restoration fund. How would that leave the Lees?'

'Without the money.'

'But if the Church's title was dubious?'

'With the money.'

'What if some Lees would sell, but others would not?'

'You mean the family might be divided on the point?'

'We do need to see the whole of the documentation to get any idea of whose the title is. How could we do that?'

'We could have a look at the original file.'

'Which is where?'

'Where you and Susan went, with Marcus More.'

'At his home. You mean he didn't give us the whole of it?'

'Seems possible, as you yourself said.'

'So we go and ask him.'

'No, I meant go and take a look when he's not about.'

Theodora thought this one over. 'Burglary?'

'Personal inquiry,' Lionel amended.

'You could end up with your brother.'

'He might value my company. On the other hand, if we could decide one way or another, that would be very pleasing.'

'And how would it help in the matter of Mick Lee's murder?'

'Now that's a separate but connected strand,' Lionel said and filled her in on the second part of Wale's tale. 'One of the little favours which Wale offered to Marcus when he was trying to get the information about the title out of him was to offer to give his no-good son a job on one of his building sites.'

'Very desirable situation in the present state of employment,' Theodora agreed.

'Particularly given young More's lack of skills.'

'And where did Leslie place him?' Theodora enquired and then suddenly realized what the answer would be.

'Yes,' said Lionel. 'As befits the son of a cleric he's supposed to be working on the cathedral restoration site.'

'So would that mean there was another person beside Leslie who had a connection with the land dispute and insider knowledge of the restoration site?'

'I imagine my Inspector Spurt will be looking at that angle,' Lionel said, 'and if he isn't, because I bet he doesn't know about the land deal background and the clergy machinations, I'll be happy to point him in the right direction.'

Theodora considered. 'First things first, however. When had you in mind to look at Marcus More's files?'

'No time like the present,' said Lionel, finishing off his dregs and scooping the rest of the nuts into his mouth.

* * *

Lionel parked his car a couple of streets from Marcus More's house. It was not Theodora's idea of a getaway car. She suggested as much to Lionel.

'Should allay suspicion, then. Anyway, Marcus and Mildred are in Chester visiting her mother till Sunday night, so we shouldn't have too much to get away from.'

'How do you know?'

'Told me to mind the shop.'

'How about the son?'

'Him we'll just have to chance. He's not the brightest of boys and with any luck he might be away carousing with his mates. Amongst his many other problems he has a drink one, I believe.'

Theodora could think of no other obstacles, so she agreed to join the raid.

Lionel, however, was (nearly) sixty-five and, therefore, chivalrous. 'You don't have to come. I know exactly what I intend to do and it really isn't necessary for you to hold the tools.'

Theodora thought of the possible effect on her own career if something went wrong. The *Church Times* headline would read FEMALE CURATE BURGLES ARCHDEACON'S HOUSE. Then she considered her career to date. 'I don't think I've much to lose,' she admitted.

Lionel got out of the car and handed her a pair of gloves, the kind available at garages for people wanting to test their oil level without getting covered in it. 'Put these on,' he said, 'then keep in close. Don't talk unnecessarily and do what I say. If we get separated go home. Don't come back to the car.'

It was a mixture of girl guides and Enid Blyton as far as Theodora was concerned. Was giggling allowed?

'What happens if the file is in a safe?' she asked before radio silence was imposed.

'I should die of amazement, knowing Marcus.'

Together they paced down the laurel and privet hedges of the Archdeacon's neighbourhood. It was quite dark at half past ten with no moon. But the heat of the day lingered in the smell of burnt grass and the smoke of autumn bonfires. Theodora felt this might be her last hour on earth. Her senses were preternaturally sharp. She was the first, therefore, to notice the police car parked at the end of the road with its lights switched off. She nudged Lionel who nodded.

'Neighbourhood watch,' he suggested, as though this had nothing to do with them.

'We're what they're watching for,' Theodora whispered.

'Not the way I do it,' said Lionel, wheeling right without warning and without varying his pace into an alleyway between two rows of houses. On either side were the plank fences of back gardens. The path was too narrow for them to walk abreast. It was muddy and there was a smell of nettle and dock as they crunched them underfoot. Theodora was wearing what she would ever afterwards think of as her housebreaking gear, thick denims and a pair of shoes suitable for fell walking. She had not felt the occasion called for a clerical collar.

About fifty yards in, Lionel stopped and counted the chimneys. Then he moved on and stopped again, counted again and felt down the planks of the right-hand fence. There was a slight rasping sound and a door made of the same planks as the fence opened inwards a couple of feet.

'You've been here before,' Theodora said accusingly.

'Time spent in reconnaissance,' Lionel said smugly, as they edged their way into the Archdeacon's vegetable garden.

There were no lights on at the back of the house. Lionel stumped confidently down the narrow grass path between decaying cabbages and neglected gooseberry bushes towards the back door, as though he owned the place. Theodora strode after him with trepidation and admiration. The back part of the Archdeacon's house was less salubrious than she remembered the front being. The dustbins were malodorous, and there was a nasty smell of uneaten cat food. This Janus tendency seemed to be a feature of the Archdeacon's life, she reflected.

Lionel was moving cautiously through the increased darkness in the shadow of the house until he reached a door a little to one side. He halted, bent down and fumbled under a brick on the ground beside the outlet of the drainpipe. Theodora realized he had a key. 'How come?' she breathed. Lionel hushed her and pushed open the door. They stopped and listened. In the distance was the sound of heavy metal thudding away. Lionel pointed upwards. Theodora understood him to mean that the noise was coming from upstairs. 'How about leaving it until another time?' Theodora said in the light of this irrefutable information.

For answer Lionel strode forward confidently. He's certainly been here before, Theodora thought, and did not know whether that was a comfort or not. One behind the other, they made their way through the kitchen. Theodora could smell stale cooking and drying tea cloths. As they came out into the hall and up to the bottom of the staircase which she remembered from her previous visit with Susan, there was the sound of a door at the top of the house opening. The music increased in volume and a ray of light came down the stairwell. Lionel's movements were not sudden but they were smart. He had both himself and Theodora flattened against the hall door beside the coat stand in one swift gesture. Theodora thought, how very good he is at this. I thought he was infantry, not SAS. From above, against the background of the music, came the sound of men's voices raised in anger and slurred by alcohol or drugs. The words, however, were not intelligible. After a moment the door swung closed again and the sounds diminished. As they did so, Lionel sprang into life and shot into the study. Theodora loped along behind him, beginning to enter into the spirit of the thing. She wasn't even surprised when Lionel took a powerful rubber torch out of his jacket and flashed it round the room. She noticed his flashing was not random but trained, designed to make sure whether the curtains were drawn (they weren't) and whether any part of the room was inhabited by anyone else (it wasn't). Then he went quickly down the drawers in the desk. He made absolutely no sound at all. He did not appear to be breathing. None yielded the file. Lionel did not pause. He motioned Theodora over to the window and without hesitation released a catch in the side of the chest which stood there. A narrow drawer slid open and Theodora could see the familiar faded blue cardboard of the files which had filled the archive room at the diocesan office. Lionel had gathered it up into his capacious jacket pocket when all hell broke loose above them.

There was a noise as of furniture being heaved about and then something which started as a laugh and turned into a scream which went on and on. No one screamed like that in civilized society. It belonged to a world of violence, of war even, which Theodora did not inhabit. There was the sound of feet stumbling down the stairs and out into the hall. The front door let in a draught of cold fresh air which could be felt even in the study. Lionel was at the study door before she could move. He flung it open and instead of, as she had supposed, making for the back door and escape, he leaped up the stairs. Theodora paused for a moment. It was then that she heard the police sirens and the sound of a number of heavy feet running over gravel. Even if she had wanted, she could not have escaped whoever was about to enter the house in large numbers so she reckoned Lionel's side was the best place to be. She took the stairs two at a time.

The room at the top of the house was designed like a studio. It stretched over the whole of the front part of the house with a picture window along one side and a skylight over a good half of the sloping ceiling. It was brightly and theatrically lit with spotlights. There was a lot of room and very little furniture. On the floor beside the sofa someone was clawing at his face and moaning. Theodora recognized the young man who had opened the door to Susan and herself a couple of days ago. Lionel had produced an immaculately white handkerchief and was busy stanching the blood. 'Hold your head *back*,' he said testily to the youth. 'It's only a flesh wound.'

'I'll get an ambulance,' Theodora said but the two uniformed police were already in the door.

'Good evening, officers,' she said composedly. 'You come in good time. Have you a mobile between you?'

Lionel looked up. 'Is Inspector Spurt with you, by any chance?'

These were country coppers not the Met, Theodora realized as soon as she saw their reaction to Lionel. They were not exactly deferential but they weren't the thuggish paramilitaries she had seen operating in her own patch in Betterhouse.

'Ah, Ted,' said Lionel as the inspector came through the door, 'I thought I saw your car at the end of the road as I came by.' Theodora's admiration for Lionel took yet another turn upwards.

'Hello, sir,' said the inspector. 'Not your usual patch, this one, is it?'

'Well, actually it rather is. This is Archdeacon More's house, as you must know.'

'I had noticed. But he's not here, I gather.'

'He's on holiday at the moment. He asked me to keep an eye on things while he and Mildred are in Chester. Feed the cat. Neighbourhood watch. Just as well Miss Braithwaite and I looked in. In the circumstances.'

'And what do you take those circumstances to be, sir?'

Theodora thought this was a good question and looked forward to the answer. Lionel looked down at the young man he was cradling in his erstwhile clean handkerchief, now reddened with his blood. 'I think the Archdeacon's son doesn't keep good company, Ted. Were you here to keep an eye on him too?'

The inspector nodded. Lionel went on, 'Did you pick up the other lad who must have been going out as you came in?'

Spurt shook his head. 'The night is young yet, sir. I think we have a good chance before the day is upon us.'

'And which of them will you be charging with the murder of Mick Lee?'

* * *

'Mrs Lure,' said Theodora, 'I wonder if you can help me with one or two matters?'

Mrs Lure deeply resented being accosted just as she was about to go home after a hard day's labour by someone she scarcely knew. She smiled her glassy smile. 'I'm sure we can work something out, Miss, er, Braithwaite, isn't it? Theodora?'

Theodora leaned across Mrs Lure's crowded desk. She felt like death after the adventures of the previous night. She and Lionel and Inspector Spurt had worked out a line of inquiry which, as Inspector Spurt had said, ought to wrap things up nicely. The only flaw as far as she could see was that it relied heavily on her skills and time rather than anyone else's. But, as Lionel said, research skills are very like detective skills and 'you have the historical knowledge and the clerical bureaucracy at your fingertips'. Theodora's hot denial of any such thing hadn't weighed with Spurt who was eager to pass the difficult bits on to her because he was undermanned, and Lionel had apparently not heard her. The result was that Theodora had spent the whole day on the phone to Kew, to Lambeth, to the local history archive of Giltchrist public library, and finally, and most triumphantly, to the Reverend Dr Gilbert Racy at St Sylvester's Foundation Betterhouse. If, therefore, she could just wrap Veronica Lure up she reckoned she'd deserve what she had promised to Susan and Lionel by way of supper.

'It concerns your collecting boxes.' Theodora set down the one she'd retrieved from the haberdashery shop of the Misses Calvert in Giltchrist high street.

'It's a very worthy cause.' Mrs Lure was pious.

'Have you collected for it long?'

'For some time.'

'About how long?'

'Time does so fly.'

'Can you tell me the procedure for placing them in shops like the Misses Calvert's?'

Mrs Lure looked shocked at the idea of going into the banausic details. 'If you want to contribute to the good cause, Miss er Braithwaite, I'm sure we need not go into the administrative procedures.'

'I'm interested in one particularly generous contributor to this particular cause. The Provost.'

'Is he? That's very good of him.'

'You weren't aware?' If Mrs Lure could simulate amazement, Theodora wasn't bad at it herself. She supposed what she was feeling was righteous indignation. This bloody woman was mocking the generosity of good people and using an altruistic system to further her own mean ends. Theodora would almost rather have the bullying and aggression of the senior clergy than this devious malice.

'Your administrative centre in,' Theodora tipped the metal container towards her and read the faded blue label, 'in Hendon says that boxes are to be collected every three months by a designated representative and forwarded to them under a seal which the society provides for them.'

'So I believe.'

'The Misses Calvert's institution is visited by you every month, usually late on Saturday afternoon just before they close. Is that so?'

'I'm a keen, some have been kind enough to say a gifted, needlewoman. The Misses Calvert's establishment is, to a connoisseur like me, a veritable garden of delights.'

'When did you last visit them?'

'Really, Miss, er, Braithwaite, I cannot recall. And, if I may say so, this is a very intrusive line of conversation. Good servant of the Church though I hope I am, my hobbies are my own.'

'It's odd you can't remember, because the Misses Calvert are both certain you looked in at lunchtime today.'

'It's possible.'

'And you took away the box, as usual?'

'I am a registered collector.'

'You *were* a registered collector,' Theodora corrected. 'They took you off the list eighteen months ago and have sent you no further boxes and no further seals. Consequently, they have received nothing from you since that date.'

'I do not have a lot of free time. I am a widow. I can give only my widow's mite.' Mrs Lure seemed to feel this concluded matters.

Theodora had enough. 'Is this the collecting box you gave to the Misses Calvert?'

Mrs Lure's expression became, if possible, even more glazed.

'Mrs Lure,' Theodora repeated, 'is this collecting box the one you allocated to the Misses Calvert?'

'It's possible. They all resemble each other, of course. I'm not sure I could tell t'other from which, if pressed.' She emphasized this last phrase to show how much she resented Theodora's unladylike activities.

'Have you yet opened the one you collected from the Misses Calvert?'

'Yes, of course I have. There was nothing in it.'

Mrs Lure realized this was an error.

'But you're supposed to send the tin sealed to Hendon.'

Mrs Lure reckoned she'd had enough. 'I don't see—'

'The Provost has been in the habit of placing a certain amount of money in this tin once a month on Saturday mornings. You have picked it up some time later. No guide dog has benefited from this transaction.'

'How do you know all this?' Mrs Lure was indignant.

Theodora tapped her finger on the bottom of the tin and allowed the loose metal cap to drop on to the desk. Then she shook the container and out tumbled a brown envelope. 'And who would you say this belonged to?'

'Really, I have not the remotest idea.'

'I'd say it belonged originally to the Provost, Reggie Tye.'

'How do you come to that conclusion?'

'It has his name and address on it,' said Theodora. 'He's a great reuser of envelopes. And for your information, Mrs Lure, I picked up the box you gave to the Misses Calvert before you visited them today, and put an empty one in its place. The one with the Provost's money in I intend to return to him.'

* * *

'Firstly, the file on St Sylvester's Cray Martyr,' Lionel said, smiling gently at Reggie Tye. 'And secondly, Wale Holdings.'

Lionel was not tired after his night's exertions. He felt very chipper, if anyone had asked him. He'd talked at some length with Inspector Spurt and agreed how to divide the clearing-up between them. 'I'll take the clergy,' Lionel had said. Spurt had seemed relieved. 'That is, I'll take the Provost and the Archdeacon if he should return from Chester in time. Theodora, I'm sure, can do the archive research stuff. And that leaves you with Wale, and the Lees.' Spurt had welcomed all that too.

So here Lionel was in the Provost's room in the cathedral office at nine thirty in the morning, showered, shaved and breakfasted, gently urging Reggie to the confessional. He glanced out of the window behind the Provost's shoulder and saw that work had been resumed on the cathedral tower.

'I'm not sure that I'm with you.' Reggie cleared his throat and reached for the Vicks inhaler and a paper handkerchief.

'I looked in last night at the Archdeacon's,' Lionel said as though he were in the habit of dropping in on his boss to socialize.

'Thought he was away.' Reggie seemed to feel this would be the end of the conversation.

'In Chester,' Lionel agreed. 'However, in the course of an interesting night's activity, I came across this file.' He slid the blue-covered file across the desk. Reggie pushed his chair backwards as though confronted with Macbeth's dagger. 'I gather you took it out early in the summer, June time. Later you passed it, I imagine on his insistence, to the Archdeacon, who incidentally in his orderly fashion signed it out of the archive room. A nicety you had failed to observe.'

'Absolutely not,' Reggie was able to reassure him.

'The Archdeacon said you did,' Lionel lied.

'I thought you said he was in Chester.' There was a whine in Reggie's tone suggesting that he'd been the victim of an unfair move.

'Miss Braithwaite and your wife saw the Archdeacon before he went away,' Lionel said. Reggie chewed this one over. He obviously knew that his wife had been to see Marcus, though Lionel doubted whether she had revealed what had passed between the three of them.

'We have to keep our hands on the ropes, our eyes on the ball, our noses to the scent. That sort of thing.' Reggie exhausted his supply of sporting metaphors. 'These developers not quite . . . *gentlemen*, to use an old-fashioned word. Nothing against Kate, of course, very useful adjunct to the management team of the cathedral. Excellent appointment,' Reggie gabbled. 'A woman,' he gasped, asserting, in Lionel's view, his first truth.

'I've read the file very carefully,' Lionel said. Then he added, 'I felt it was part of my duties as the Archdeacon's assistant.' His tone was virtuous to the point of piety. Two could play at this game of advertising conscientiousness, he reckoned. 'You were looking at the file with a view, I take it, to determining the ownership of the land behind the church and school in Cray Martyr.'

Reggie cleared his throat and blew his nose on the inadequate paper handkerchief. Then he nodded.

'Good,' said Lionel, genuinely pleased. At last they were beginning to make progress. 'The cathedral,' he went on with apparent inconsequence, 'is not exactly a beautiful building but it has presence. It ought to be preserved, you feel?'

'I'm not going to let it fall down in my time,' Reggie agreed. 'We have a duty to posterity,' he added heavily.

What a bore he is, Lionel thought. He's gone to all this trouble and caused all this bother because he can't bear to be blamed.

'I was especially interested in this document,' Lionel went on. 'Its handwriting, your handwriting, is very handsome. A legal copperplate, is it not?'

Reggie sneezed and busied himself with repairing the damage to his person caused by this. Lionel understood him to say that he didn't know what Lionel was talking about.

'What I'm talking about is your forging a document to show that the land behind the church and school at Cray Martyr belonged to the Church, that the Lees were merely tenants, and that when their tenancy ended or if they changed the use of the land from what the agreement specified, that land reverted to the original trustees, namely the charitable Foundation of St Sylvester.'

Reggie could bear this no longer. 'The Foundation of St Sylvester transferred the trusteeship to the Provost and Chapter of Giltchrist Cathedral in nineteen seventeen.'

'So I gathered,' Lionel said equably. 'There's what looks like a perfectly genuine transfer document. No, the one I think is forged is this one.' Lionel tapped the paper under Reggie's nose. 'All I want to know is why you concocted it.'

'You've absolutely no shred of proof,' Reggie said with an unexpected show of spirit.

'Any forensic test of the paper and ink would show when and by whom this could have been written.' Lionel was not too sure that this was true but he wasn't going to let Reggie off the hook without a fight.

There was a moment's pause. Lionel thought he ought to help this helpless man to make a start so he offered, 'Wale

Holdings approached you about the sale of the land for Mackenzie's All Foods, yes?'

Reggie nodded.

'Sir Derek Thing from English Heritage offered—'

'Pound for pound,' Reggie repeated the magic phrase, 'for the cathedral restoration fund. Yes.'

'Such an opportunity might not occur again,' Lionel concluded for him. 'And the Archdeacon?'

'Marcus reckoned that he ought to handle the Wale Holdings side of things. He said,' Reggie reddened at the memory, 'that Wale was a shark and he'd do better than me with him.'

Lionel leaned across the table. 'So who killed Mick Lee and why?'

'It was an accident,' said Reggie stubbornly.

'No it wasn't,' said Lionel. There was a moment's pause and then Lionel resumed. 'I had an interesting session with Leslie Wale yesterday. I went there thinking that Wale arranged the killing of Mick Lee in order to make it easier to negotiate with Deke, because Wale believed that the land belonged to the Lees. I also thought that Deke Lee was chasing Leslie and indeed Kate because he thought that Wale had killed his brother. But . . .' Lionel stopped.

'But Wale knew that the land didn't belong to the Lees, it belonged to the Church. I told him so when he saw me in June.'

'Exactly.' Lionel was triumphant. 'So Wale had no motive for killing Mick Lee. Wale thinks that Deke was hounding himself and Kate because he thought that Wale had the proof that the land belonged to the Church and that his own lease had ended.'

'Why on earth should he think that? I mean, think that Wale had the Church's title documents?'

'I wonder,' said Lionel, 'where Archdeacon More is at this moment?'

Reggie caught his meaning.

'The police will question the Archdeacon,' Lionel pressed home his advantage. 'I doubt if he'll protect you, would you say?'

Reggie thought about that. He blew his nose one last time, hawked into his handkerchief and prepared to make a clean breast of things.

* * *

'It's terribly kind of you to cook breakfast for supper,' Susan Tye said to Theodora, contemplating the *richesse* of bacon, liver, kidneys, sausages, fried tomatoes, fried mushrooms, fried bread, fried eggs.

'It's the only meal I can cook,' Theodora admitted.

'The best meal the English do.' Lionel, at any rate, was appreciative.

'What's this?' Susan asked, nudging a large thick lump of something towards the edge of her plate.

'Black pudding,' said Lionel. 'Don't wreck it. I'll eat it, if you don't want it.'

Lionel seemed to have been renewed in vigour since his success in burgling his boss's house. Theodora filled the toast rack as it should be filled with a mixture of rounds of thick wholemeal toast and thin white ones. It had been a real pleasure to go down Giltchrist high street that morning, on her way to the Misses Calvert's, gathering the wherewithal for a decent meal. Cooper's Oxford lay side by side with Kentish honey. The remains of the squeezed oranges were stacked on the draining board in the kitchen of the Provost's Lodging. There was the smell of fresh coffee percolating on the stove. Bet it's never seen the like before, Theodora thought to herself. The spaniel graced them with his presence and sat next to Lionel, drooling.

'So what happened when you saw your sergeant?'

'Inspector,' Lionel said. 'I have to say he was very civil, given that we have rather poached in his neck of the woods.'

'He said something about the clerical systems being impenetrable and so it was quite useful to get specialist help in that area.' Lionel smiled at Theodora and offered toast.

'What about that snake Veronica Lure?' Susan was unforgiving of her husband's tormentor.

'Depends what they can make stick in the way of blackmail charges.'

'But she admitted she was guilty to Theo.'

'People have a habit of retracting what they've confessed to at later dates.'

'It will depend too on how much Reggie wants to press charges. Particularly in the light of . . .' Lionel was going to say Reggie's own dubious conduct, but remembered in time that he wasn't sure just how much Susan knew about her husband's dubious activities.

He need not have worried. Susan's loyalty to Reggie was made of the finest metal. 'It doesn't matter what Reggie has done. If need be we must sue the woman privately. She must be stopped.'

Lionel thought how very nice the office would be without Mrs Lure, how much faster his letters would go out and how he wouldn't have to keep flattering and cajoling. 'How was she actually doing it?' he asked Theodora.

'She left a collecting box with the Misses Calvert and picked it up once a month when Reggie had dropped his thousand in it after he'd been to the post office.'

'Wouldn't he look a bit out of place in a haberdashery?' Lionel objected.

'Collar studs,' said Theodora succinctly.

'Not much worn nowadays, given the death of the detachable collar,' Lionel agreed.

'And, of course, easily lost and so needing constant replacement,' Susan admitted.

'At least once a month.'

'Poor, poor Reggie. How could she, the ghastly old besom? Just because Reggie made one or two errors of judgement.'

Theodora looked at Lionel. Lionel was not disposed to acquiesce in Susan's view of things. 'Reggie deliberately falsified legal documents,' he said.

'But he did it for the sake of the Church,' Susan objected.

Theodora thought Lionel was going to say that Reggie's falsifications were so amateurish that they deserved to be exposed. However, he compromised with, 'Ends don't justify means.'

Theodora wondered whether Susan was quite up to that sort of concept.

'As far as I can see,' Susan said, 'all Reggie did was to put in writing the ownership of a strip of land which undoubtedly *had been* the Church's but which the Lees wouldn't let go of. And he did it for the best possible motive because that food firm wouldn't give him any money for his cathedral unless they could have access to the land and the Church would give them access. But the Lees were a maverick lot and wouldn't have let it go out of sheer perversity.'

Susan stopped. She'd delivered her narrative without punctuation, under the pressure of her eagerness to get it clear to herself and make it clear to her audience that Reggie wasn't at fault.

'Depends what you mean by "put in writing".' Theodora didn't want to cause Susan pain but she'd spent a whole day chasing through land registries trying to trace documents relating to that piece of land. Reggie's casual forgery of a letter showing that the land had originally had a reverter on it had been a considerable time-waster.

'But really and truly,' Susan said, 'really and truly the land did belong to the Church, so there was no reason why Reggie shouldn't make that a teeny weeny bit clearer and get his money from the food people to finance the cathedral restoration.'

'It all depends on what you mean by "the Church".' Lionel was all set to be judicious.

'Well, we're all one, at heart,' Susan objected.

'The Church might equal the diocese, or the vicar and churchwardens of St Sylvester's, or the heirs of the original donors, i.e. the Foundation of St Sylvester,' said Theodora, who knew.

'It's all the same in the end,' Susan objected.

'No,' said Theodora and Lionel together.

'If it had belonged to the diocese in the first place and they had rented it to the Lees and there were a reverter on it, it would have been straightforward,' Lionel explained. 'As soon as it was apparent that the Lees no longer used it for the purpose for which it was leased to them, it would have been easy for the diocese to claim it back and they could then sell it with a clear title to MAF.'

'And use the money for the cathedral, I suppose,' Susan said.

'Actually no.' Theodora thought she might as well impart as much elementary law to Susan as possible; you never knew when it might turn out useful, if you were married to Reggie. 'Actually it would be trust money and couldn't be donated as a gift to another trust. It would have to be used under trust law to maximize profit for the beneficiaries of the trust.'

'Who?'

'It would go into that ever open and never properly accountable maw known as diocesan funds.' Lionel should know.

'So what you're saying is that even with Reggie's, er, efforts he wouldn't have got the profits for his restoration fund?'

'Right.'

'And of course Marcus More knew that. That was why he hung on to the file — he was trying to work out some devious way of getting the money for the cathedral.' Lionel was particularly pleased by this angle of things.

'Did Marcus know who owned the land?' Susan asked.

'And how did he become aware that MAF would pay a lot of money for it?' Theodora added.

'He didn't initially, until after Wale contacted the chapter. Then he took out the file, read it and realized the Church's title might not be as clear as was desirable.'

'And not long after Reggie knew too and Reggie was told by Sir Sandy that he'd get a big contribution for his cathedral fund if he could prove title.'

'So he set to work to prove it.'

'Bless him,' said Susan.

As though he was just a lovable innocent, Theodora thought. 'How did Mrs Lure twig that Reggie was trying his hand at forgery?'

'She wanders around a bit and she'd found some of Reggie's earlier practice efforts in the archive room. Extracted one such and compared it with what was in the file. Soon after that Marcus More took the file from Reggie. So she had Reggie over a barrel both ways.' Lionel had ceased to moderate his language to spare Susan's feelings. 'Reggie didn't want Marcus to know that one of the crucial documents in the file was forged. Nor did he want MAF to know that.'

'So he paid her a thousand a month via Guide Dogs for the Blind to keep mum.'

'He's so generous,' Susan said.

I suppose that's one way of coping with being married to a fool, Theodora thought.

'So what about the Lees?' Susan went on.

'Tobias Angel knew about local land developments. He'd been clued up when the original bypass had been mooted. He reckoned local interests outweighed national or diocesan ones. He wanted the Lees to have it. He knew the land wasn't owned by the vicar and churchwardens of St Sylvester's. He didn't know it wasn't the diocese's. He hoped it might be the Lees' since they certainly thought they'd got a lease on it, something about acquiring title by adverse possession. Yes?' Lionel, Theodora realized, quite liked this sort of layman law.

'So what's adverse possession?' Susan asked.

'It's when the landlord forgets to enforce his rights or renew them and the tenant continues over time to enjoy them,' Theodora explained. 'In the end and in some circumstances the mere enjoyment of the right gives title.'

'So,' Lionel was pressing on, 'Angel told the Lees that someone was after the land, and when Wale asked Vincent to see if the Lees had title and would they sell, Angel urged them not to but to hang on.'

'As he told them to do in the case of the bypass,' Theodora said.

'Right. So Vincent started negotiations with the Lees and got as far as Jon Lee who thought he had the title deeds but couldn't read them.'

'So he wanted Father Tobias to have a look before he handed them to anyone else. And that's what they were doing the night of the accident.' Susan contributed her mite.

'Right. But before Jon could get the deeds to Tobias to read he was killed.'

'So who was responsible for that?'

'Almost certainly Deke. Father Tobias spoke about a family feud.' Lionel looked at Theodora. 'Deke didn't reckon he wanted anyone getting their eyes on his deeds, or what he thought of as his deeds.'

'He has a superstitious attitude to bits of paper?' Theodora suggested.

'Comes of not being able to read them.'

'So he took them off his brother after he'd killed him and hung on. But in fact Deke only has the earlier lease on his land, he doesn't have the original title deeds.'

'Then when Wale took up the chase for them from Vincent, he approached Mick Lee, as being the more user-friendly of the two remaining brothers. The only difficulty for Mick was he didn't know where Deke kept the bits he had.'

'Did his son, Henry, know?' Susan asked in a sudden inspiration.

'Henry is a lad of parts who listens to adult conversation. He knew that you're buried with important documents and reckoned he could help his dad by tracking down the papers.'

'He's been searching the tombs of St Andrew's,' Theodora explained.

‘Why St Andrew’s and not St Sylvester’s?’

‘Previous Lees have been buried there,’ said Lionel. ‘It’s the traditional travellers’ burial ground. The fact that they haven’t been laid to rest there for over a century wouldn’t be all that clear to Henry.’

‘What a very brave little boy,’ said Susan in admiration. ‘But he didn’t find the deeds, then?’

Lionel looked at Theodora. ‘No,’ he said.

‘So who’s got them?’ Susan asked.

‘Actually I have them,’ Theodora admitted.

‘I always knew I could trust you,’ Susan said with admiration.

‘Well, not me personally, of course. But our foundation, the Foundation of St Sylvester at Betterhouse, has a complete set of all the title deeds of all the considerable amount of land which Thomas Henry Newcome gave to the Church in the Cray Martyr area. Gilbert Racy, the current warden,’ she explained to Susan, ‘can produce them when needed.’

‘But what about poor Mick Lee?’ Susan pursued.

‘Deke via young More,’ Lionel said.

‘Oh, poor Marcus,’ Susan exclaimed.

Theodora thought that was exactly the proper response. ‘Can you prove it, though?’ she asked Lionel.

‘Spurt thinks he can. Ultimately, Deke is the only person who believed till the end that the Lees’ title may have been a good one. He also knew that young More needed cash.’

‘To get away from his father, I suppose,’ said Susan. ‘Well, anyway, that leaves Reggie in the clear. And it will be such a relief for Kate.’

‘So that makes it all right,’ Theodora said. But irony wasn’t part of Susan’s equipment.

SERMON: SUCCESS AND FAILURE

The Bishop, tanned and distinguished, a successful fifty-year-old with a mane of carefully trimmed hair and an isolated beard on his chin, newly returned from Jedda, Los Angeles and Edinburgh, smiled his nice smile at his young audience. He'd been told to wear a bit of purple for the interest of the pupils and had splendidly obliged with a purple silk cassock and a chunky silver pectoral cross. Before beginning, he handed his pastoral staff to his chaplain, who held it in an abstracted way as though he were an umbrella stand.

The Bishop looked a bit lonely out there at the front of the school hall, Lionel thought. But as he seized the wooden reading stand, thoughtfully provided by the headteacher, and relocated it with a manly gesture, Lionel realized that here was a personality who would fill the hall. He was not put off by the teachers stationed at intervals round the sides of the room like, Lionel remembered, the warders in the visitors' room at Fordingham. The pupils seated on the floor in front of him seemed to inspire him.

'Hello, everybody,' he bellowed.

But the pupils were not to be tempted. They'd been groomed, as the staff put it to each other.

'Good morning, Bishop,' they chanted.

Theodora, Lionel's guest, was seated on an infant-sized chair beside him, her long legs not far from her chin. She surveyed the scene from the viewpoint of someone who was a governor of her own St Sylvester's school in her parish in Betterhouse. The hall was no different from other primary school halls. There was a piano buttressing the Bishop on one side and a vase of flowers which looked as though it was not normally there on a table at the other. Round the walls were fixed climbing bars for the gymnasts.

The pupils here were cleaner than in Betterhouse. Some looked kempt and cosseted more than her own: the Gainshurst contingent, presumably. The others, from Cray Martyr, looked as though they'd been washed and ironed for the occasion. But really, she thought, the difference between them is slight. The uniform dress, red sweatshirts and grey skirts or trousers, perhaps even the uniform curriculum, was lessening, at least on festal occasions, the gap between the cultures. Was that a good thing, the destruction of inequality, or a bad one, the destruction of diversity?

'I have recently been abroad,' the Bishop was saying in his pleasant south London accent overlaid by time at Cambridge. 'Who knows what "abroad" means?'

Oh dear, Theodora thought, he's going to interact. She just hoped that he wasn't going to demand a map and spend time pointing out where he'd been to pupils none of whom beyond the first row could have discerned the countries and most of whom below the age of ten wouldn't know what a map was anyhow. In Theodora's experience there was a nineteenth-century missionary inside many a modern Bishop, just longing for a lantern slide and an epidiascope. But hands shot up. Pupils had been primed. Orlando Groom had done his stuff.

'Out of England.'

'Out of the UK.'

'Overseas,' came the humanities-instructed answers.

'On holiday,' said one unwise boy.

'Oh, no! It's not been a *holiday*,' said the Bishop quickly and firmly. Too many of his senior management team were inclined to think that. He'd had to teach them different. 'I've been working very, very hard.'

The boy looked as though he might be going to argue the toss about this, but Orlando Groom stooped down beside him and smiled forcefully into his face and he thought better of it.

'No. I've been meeting a great many different people from many different walks of life. People who live very differently from us. Some of them are very poor.' The Bishop paused to let the enormity of poverty sink into the assembly. 'Some of them don't have cars. Some of them don't have lavatories. Some of them don't have enough to eat.'

Some of the Cray Martyr pupils thought they could empathize with all that.

'And do you know what we talked about when we met each other?'

An unwise question, Theodora and Lionel thought together.

'Cars?' asked one.

'Lavatories?' asked another.

'Food,' said a chubby lad near the front.

The Bishop laughed heartily. 'No, no and no,' he said with real pleasure.

'I know, I know,' said a girl halfway down the hall waving her hand round her head in circles.

'Come on then,' said the Bishop as though she were a prize fighter.

'Jesus,' she cried triumphantly. She'd been right before with that answer, indeed she'd found it worked with practically any invited stranger who took school worship. No point in not trying her luck here with this one in fancy dress.

'No, sorry, not quite right. Good try, though. No, we met to talk about,' he paused, 'heaven.'

There was a perceptible drop in interest. He'd have to do more than wear fancy dress and have a beard to recover from a turn-off like that. Most of the staff realized this, geared themselves to red alert level and stepped up their crowd control techniques.

'Have any of you ever scaled a ladder?' The mighty one pressed on with that apparent inconsequentialism which either makes or mars, according to your taste, so many modern sermons. Theodora, who had heard a great many in her time, realized that the Bishop was about to embark on what musicians designate the second theme. Pupils, who did not always have the benefit of total conceptual coherence in their teachers' exposition of topics, changed gear more easily than their elders might have done. They had lower expectations.

'Yes, I have. My dad does a lot up ladders.'

'Well done,' said the Bishop heartily. 'You'll know all about what you have to do to get up a ladder. You tell us.'

'You've got to be very careful,' said the careful youth.

'Right. And you have to go a step at a time. But if you do, you get higher and higher and higher.'

Oh, God, thought Lionel, when will this end?

'And when you get to the top you have a . . .' The Bishop stopped to let the audience in.

'Dizzy,' agreed a couple of girls in the front row.

'Good view of next door,' said the lad who had a father in ladders.

'Right,' shouted the Bishop, overjoyed. 'Now, I want you to think very carefully about the next question.' The Bishop was clearly winning because his audience actually looked as though they were listening. 'Have any of you shot an arrow?'

A third theme is too much, Theodora thought. He should have used the ladder to take us to heaven and been thankful they haven't run riot. It'll end in tears.

'Arrow?' wheedled the Bishop. He made a pantomime of stretching a bow, aiming and shooting. 'Darts and arrows,' he ventured further.

'I've played darts,' said a cultivated voice from the Gainshurst neck of the woods. 'With my cousin,' it added as though to explain his departure from more usual pastimes.

'Right.' The Bishop was duly thankful. As so he should be, thought Lionel.

'Now,' said the Bishop, 'I'm going to make a comparison.'

Let's hope to heaven he's not going to ask them what a comparison is or we'll be here all night, was the united thought of the staff.

'Heaven is a code name for success. Heaven is like the top of a ladder or hitting the bull's eye in darts or the centre of the target with a bow and arrow. It's what we all want to do. We all want to reach the top of the tree. We all want to hit the mark. What I'd like you boys and girls to do is to think when you go out of here today, what am I aiming at? Where is my success? Am I a ladder person or a bull's eye person? And what do I really want to reach?' The Bishop seemed to feel he had made his point. He smiled and raised his hand to give a blessing.

A number of lads in the back rows were miming stretching bows and throwing darts. They knew what they were for. Nothing like a good fight. Nothing like beating someone else.

'I don't think I agree with him,' Lionel whispered to Theodora.

'No,' she agreed, gazing at the turbulence amongst the pupils, 'he's got it all quite wrong.'

THE END

THE JOFFE BOOKS STORY

We began in 2014 when Jasper agreed to publish his mum's much-rejected romance novel and it became a bestseller.

Since then we've grown into the largest independent publisher in the UK. We're extremely proud to publish some of the very best writers in the world, including Joy Ellis, Faith Martin, Caro Ramsay, Helen Forrester, Simon Brett and Robert Goddard. Everyone at Joffe Books loves reading and we never forget that it all begins with the magic of an author telling a story.

We are proud to publish talented first-time authors, as well as established writers whose books we love introducing to a new generation of readers.

We have been shortlisted for Independent Publisher of the Year at the British Book Awards three times, in 2020, 2021 and 2022, and for the Diversity and Inclusivity Award at the Independent Publishing Awards in 2022.

We built this company with your help, and we love to hear from you, so please email us about absolutely anything bookish at: feedback@joffebooks.com

If you want to receive free books every Friday and hear about all our new releases, join our mailing list: www.joffebooks.com/contact

And when you tell your friends about us, just remember: it's pronounced Joffe as in coffee or toffee!

ALSO BY D.M. GREENWOOD

THEODORA BRAITHWAITE MURDER MYSTERIES

Printed in Great Britain
by Amazon

22152246R00118